Orange Blossom Café

T.I. LOWE

ISBN: 9781074575076

Lynn Weldon, thanks for helping me come up with a proper Louisianan last name for Phillip Moreau.

&

Lynn Edge. Well shine, my friend, I love you and am thankful for the sunshine you've added to my life.

Also by T.I. LOWE

Lulu's Café

Any Given Moment

Goodbyes and Second Chances

Coming Home Again

Julia's Journey

A Discovery of Hope

A Bleu Streak Christmas

A Bleu Streak Summer

Until I Do

Until I Don't

Until I Decide

~ ACKNOWLEDGEMENTS ~

A special thank you to my lovely readers. Your enthusiasm over my stories and unwavering support touches my heart more than I can express in words.

My honest and dependable beta readers, Sally Anderson, Trina Cooke, Lynn Edge, Linda Saylor, and Jennifer Strickland. Thanks for your guidance in making this story better.

My Lowe family, Bernie, Nate, and Lydia, you are my sunshine and my caramels. You make my life brighter and sweeter. Love ya!

I must thank my medical expert chick, Christy Anderson, for always answering my weird medical questions.

My Savior Jesus Christ, thank You for being the lamp to my feet and the light to this blessed writing path.

~☼**Part 1**☼~

Chapter One

Life Recipe
Take one heaping portion of common sense, two wishful
scoops of dreams (okay to add an extra scoop when needed),
and a manageable portion of drive. Mix in equal pinches of
self-respect, dignity, integrity, faith, and compassion.
Recipe Tip: If for some reason this doesn't turn out
properly, simply start recipe over, being mindful to not
make the same mistake twice.

The turquoise water of the Gulf Coast glittered with secrets and allure in the bright Florida sun as the powdery sand kept its mysteries at bay. Every so often, a palm tree would rustle out a welcome as the wind rushed by and graced it. With her toes buried within the warmth of the sand while admiring the view, Aiden O'Connell declared the moment as complete perfection.

That is until the clamoring and pinging and raucous racket from next door tore through the tranquil breeze, effectively ruining her day. Annoyance climbed on her shoulders and got comfortable as the redhead stormed off the beach in disgust.

As she slammed the back entrance door to the

Orange Blossom Café, Aiden yelled, "Why am I being punished?"

"You realize the front can hear you whining, right?" Nora asked, reminding Aiden the lunch crowd was still lingering.

Aiden huffed as she gathered her wild waves in a knot on top of her head. She eyed Nora, who was in the midst of juicing a basket of oranges for their famous marinade. Her dearest friend since freshman year of high school had hair Aiden would steal in a heartbeat if such a thing was possible to do. Always glossy and smooth in a low bun while working, or down and sleek with not even one lock daring to frizz or lay uneven when away from the kitchen. Aiden shook her head and glanced away. Tying the messy knot quickly with the ever-present band from her wrist, she made her way over to the sink.

"That crowd out there doesn't mind my sassing. The only thing that would run them out of here is if the place caught fire."

Nora eyed her sternly, always the designated sound of reason in the pair. "Do you think it's very wise to say that, beings that you've already challenged, 'Why am I being punished'?" The dark-haired beauty threw her hands in the air and mocked her friend dramatically.

"Probably not," Aiden muttered, pausing in her task of haphazardly tossing dishes in the dishwasher—another thing Nora did totally opposite of her.

Nora Bailey was all about tidiness and order.

4

Aiden didn't care so much as long as it got done. Aiden eyed the giant stainless steel machine, remembering the day it arrived. It was the first of the very few changes she mandated the moment Aunt Donna signed the café over to her a little over two years ago. It still felt like just yesterday when her Florida native aunt did the opposite of most retirees— she left the sunny warmth of the south and moved to the coolness up north.

Not many other changes had occurred since then… That is until now. The loud high-pitch buzz of a saw from next door racked the spitfire's nerves, renewing her fury.

"Aunt Donna managed all thirty years of being proprietor of this café without having to deal with mess such as this!" The volume of her husky voice rose with each word, matching the noise from outside as Aiden waved in that direction. Nora kept to the juicing task, seemingly ignoring the little temper tantrum of her company. Blowing an escaped curl out of her face, Aiden shut the dishwasher door and set it on a washing cycle.

"What is this? Some kind of Irish turf war?" Nora glanced over, finally acknowledging all of the heavy sighs escaping the redhead.

Nora loved to rib Aiden about all things Irish, and in return, Aiden liked to harass her about being a Jamaican jerk, being that the girl never spared her friend's feelings over honesty.

"Are we going to go there today?" Aiden asked sardonically.

5

"You know you're not entitled to hold other restaurants off of this strip of the coast. Stop being so *dramatic.*" Her island cadence slipped into the last word.

Conceding, Aiden made her way to the front of the café to help out the waitresses. Entering the dining area where customers lazily munched on their citrus-themed dishes while conversing with other patrons, she brushed off the annoyance and focused on her pride and joy. Aiden considered this place her home, with it carefully holding most of her thirty-three years of life.

It held her first, albeit unfulfilling, job as dishwasher—hence the dishwasher addition.

Her first overly supervised date under the watchful eyes of her parents and Aunt Donna.

The hidden memory of her first kiss on the back deck where no watchful eyes caught it except for the ocean and sand, and they never told a soul.

The bitter hurt of her first breakup that seemed to always echo from the kitchen on stormy nights where her fifteen-year-old self sobbed on Aunt Donna's shoulder.

Celebrations of birthdays, prom night pictures, graduation...

Disappointments of not making the cheerleading squad, her parents' decision to move back to Ireland after her graduation with her making the difficult but right choice to stay in Florida, the college rejection letter...

The annoying rhythm of hammering nudged the

memories away and pushed her feet to move past the front counter and away from disappointments she could do nothing about.

Aiden glanced over at the large-scaled orange images boldly dressing the grey-teak shiplap walls, remembering the day she hung them. Some were of just the delicate white blossoms while others held the vividly bright fruit itself. She kept the images of bountiful orange groves that Aunt Donna already had adorning the walls. It only felt right to mingle the old with the new with wanting to honor the legacy her aunt had founded in this ultimate breakfast and lunch venue.

Aiden stopped reminiscing, a habit as of late which she totally blamed on the epic change roaring loudly from just outside, and began weaving through the cream-colored tables. Happy contentment twinkled along her hazel eyes as she chatted with customers and helped the waitresses with keeping the glasses generously filled. Nora was the kitchen expert while Aiden's social expertise shined in the front, making the young ladies the perfect team.

As the lunch rush was beginning to ebb, the front door opened, causing Aiden to halt in the task of refilling a customer's glass with orange tea. The stranger holding his head down while heading to the counter had completely stolen her attention as well as her ability to move. Never had a threadbare T-shirt and frayed shorts looked so appealing.

Sure, Aiden had seen her share of good looking men in her life. She even agreed to marry one before she abruptly came to her senses just days before the wedding. The locals deemed her commitment gun-shy and the town's runaway bride, so no other proposal had been offered since that unfortunate one six years ago. Never one to smear a name, Aiden bravely allowed everyone to believe what they wanted while keeping her ex-fiancé's indiscretions to herself—another secret the walls of the café loyally held. Neal was long gone, but the bruise he inflicted never quite healed all the way.

Aiden watched on as her new waitress Brittany placed a menu on the counter in front of the stranger. He said something to elicit a giggle from the young blonde. She offered him a flirty smile before disappearing into the kitchen.

Feeling overly hospitable all of a sudden, Aiden stepped around the counter. "Welcome to the Orange Blossom Café." The husky note of her voice came out more pronounced, but she didn't dare clear her throat.

The man lifted his eyes from the menu and peered at her from underneath the brim of his tattered ball cap. A smile bloomed across his friendly face, reminding Aiden of the radiant sunshine she witnessed on the beach earlier.

He offered his hand. "I'm Phillip Moreau. New in town."

She took it. "Aiden O'Connell. Local and part-owner of this café."

His smile turned up several notches to a full-on grin as he glanced around. "No kidding."

He had yet to release her hand, so she gently tugged it free and grabbed an order pad. "What can I get you?" As she asked this, Brittany pushed through the kitchen door, looking a bit disappointed. Aiden offered her a shrug, conveying *you gotta be quicker than that*. The young waitress relented and moved over to collect a table's check.

"Hmm..." the handsome murmured, drawing her attention back to him, as he scanned the menu. "What's the best dish on the menu?"

She couldn't hold back the laugh. "Mr. Moreau, that's like asking a mother to pick her favorite child. That's a big no-no."

"Call me Fisher. And I promise not to tell the other selections." He nodded sincerely, pressing his pouty lips together to hold back a smile.

Aiden regarded his full lips for a few beats too long before refocusing on his friendly eyes. "Fisher?" She tapped her pen against the pad.

"Yeah. Third generation fisherman. My gramps nicknamed me that 'cause I could hold a fishing pole before I began walking." An understated lilt whispered through his words.

"Louisianan?" she guessed.

"Yes, ma'am. Born and raised, but I'll be relocating here in the next few months."

Aiden caught a few patrons lifting their hands to wave goodbye to her, so she returned the gesture while asking, "So are you retiring from fishing?" Clearly he was too young to retire from anything, but she wanted to be nosy without being too obvious.

"Moreau men never retire from fishing. I'm bringing my boat and crew here."

She wanted to continue the line of questions, but reined in her curiosity and pointed to her favorite dish on the menu.

"Pan-seared Red Snapper with citrus salsa," he read, sounding intrigued. "I'll have that."

She jotted the order on the pad, offered him a smile, and hurried to place his order, knowing Nora probably had most of the kitchen already cleaned.

Sure enough, Nora was wiping the grill top down while glaring at the paper Aiden tried offering her. "It's closing time. I already told Brittany no."

When Nora made no move to accept the order, Aiden placed the ticket on a clamp along the edge of the grill hood. She then glimpsed the time on the clock above the kitchen door.

Yep, closing time.

"It's for a new customer. Be nice and I'll make it up to you." Aiden blew her glowering friend a kiss before grabbing Fisher a glass of iced tea and bolting out of the kitchen.

By the time Fisher's order was ready, the dining area had completely cleared except for the waitresses cleaning the day's success away. The closed sign had been placed on the glass front door and the curtains closed, yet Aiden and her handsome new customer seemed content to linger in each other's company.

His looked appreciatively at the plate as she slid it in front of him. The confetti of citrus salsa, consisting of various orange and grapefruit diced and married with olive oil and chopped mint, complimented the perfectly seared fish. "Wow. This is... Wow."

Aiden felt the same way, but her eyes were trained on him and not the dish.

From Fisher's savory ocean scent to his bronzed complexion and gold eyes, Aiden had no doubt the sun kissed him before bathing him in the sea. He was undeniably a beautiful creation born directly from sunshine and surf.

Aiden gravitated closer to him and whispered in an accusing tone, "Did you allow the sun to kiss you?"

A hint of mischief twinkled in his molten eyes as the side of his mouth kicked up slightly. He glanced around the café before leaning over the counter, which successfully eliminated a few more inches between them. Dipping his head and peeking up from under the brim of his hat, he answered, "I've never been one to kiss and tell."

Then, when Aiden didn't think she could be drawn to him any further, the man took off his hat and ran a hand through a mess of brown and gold waves. With neatly trimmed sides, there was no evidence such a lush head of hair was hidden underneath that unassuming hat. She blinked away the sun and sea and was now in a world of chocolate and caramel. Talk about sensory overload.

Entranced, she absently wiped the counter down more times than needed, and managed the leisureliest floor sweep behind the counter in the history of the café while keeping him company. He seemed in no hurry either, taking his sweet time eating. Her over-cleaning of the counter eventually drew his gold eyes to it.

He smoothed his hand over the shiny countertop surface. "This is a pretty unique idea."

Aiden smiled as she perused the collage of vintage orange crate labels. Each one unique and brightly colored, sealed underneath a thick layer of clear epoxy. "My aunt is a closet artist. She designed this place and was the owner for the first thirty years of its existence."

"So you have a sense of family tradition, too," Fisher commented while looking around. His gaze paused on the large driftwood sign hanging over the door. The words swirled in an understated hue of orange. "She made that, too?"

"She did," Aiden confirmed while silently reading the verse it held.

Offer hospitality to one another without grumbling. 1Peter 4:9

"I'm really digging this place." Fisher nodded his head with conviction before taking the final bite of fish. "This is over-the-top good. Seriously, the best Red Snapper dish I've ever had." He collected the last forkful of the salsa, taking his time savoring it before swallowing. "You think this would be good with Mahi-Mahi?"

Aiden shrugged. "I don't see why not."

"You wouldn't share the recipe with me, would ya?" That pouty smile slowly returned.

Aiden narrowed her eyes at him, realizing that

little look had to be Fisher's personal lure. Aiden saw no reason to not share it for a small favor in return. "If you promise to share some fresh Mahi-Mahi when they come into season."

"It's a deal." He amped up that grin while offering his hand to seal the deal.

Aiden happily shook it, but when she tried to take her hand back this time, Fisher didn't oblige. He pulled her closer in his direction. If he kept on, she would have no choice but to climb on top of the counter. Her feet were barely touching the floor at that point. She didn't find the idea unappealing at all.

His lips began to move at some point, but the heartbeat dancing in her ears caused her to miss the words. She said nothing until his voice finally registered.

"Aiden?" he whispered.

She managed to rasp out a garbled, "Yes?"

"Would you write the recipe down for me?"

She blinked out of the haze and pulled away from him, disappointment prickling her skin. Clearing her throat, she managed a head nod before scurrying into the little office off the left side of the kitchen. She plopped the severely worn recipe card on top of the printer and hit the copy button, nearly blinding herself due to forgetting to close the lid. Rubbing the dots away from her vision, she headed back to the only customer in the café and handed him the copy along with his check without looking anywhere near the fishing deity's captivating glamour.

"You forgot something," Fisher called out just as

she was about to go hide in the kitchen until he magically disappeared.

"What's that?" Aiden asked over her shoulder, hand still resting on the door, as she noticed him studying the recipe.

"This recipe is no good."

She spun around and perched her hands on her hips. "And why's that?"

He watched her closely as the mischievous glint reappeared in his golden eyes. "It doesn't have your phone number. It's no good without it." He pushed the paper across the counter without releasing her from his gaze.

Heat bloomed across her checks while she bit back the smile that demanded its freedom. To regain her bearings, she pulled on her armor of sass. "The recipe is perfect just the way it is. My advice is to not fool with it."

"Your name suits you," he said appreciatively.

"And how do you know what my name means?" She narrowed her eyes.

"I looked it up on my phone while waiting for my food. It means *little fire*."

Well, if that didn't impress her, she didn't know what would. Fisher taking the time to search her name meaning showed genuine interest. Her nature wouldn't normally allow her to give in so easily, but before it protested, Aiden scribbled her number on the recipe copy. Some little tickle in the back of her mind whispered its disapproval for fooling with her life recipe. She scratched along her neck to rid the tickle, thinking enough time had passed since she allowed a man her number, and maybe that recipe was due a tweaking.

By the time Fisher polished off his third glass of tea, settled the bill, and sauntered out the door with her number and her interest, Aiden felt weak-kneed. Plopping down on the stool he just vacated, she finally noticed Nora standing by the kitchen door with an eyebrow raised with wanting to know the scoop on what that was all about. Having no desire to give her friend any response due to not understanding it herself, Aiden hopped down and made a beeline to the exit.

"Where are you going?" Nora called out from behind her.

Without turning around, she muttered, "I'm going to the sweet shop across the street. I've suddenly got a mad craving for chocolate dipped caramels."

The tinkling laughter of the few remaining waitresses and Nora followed Aiden out the door, but she disregarded it and focused on her absurd hunger for something sweet.

Chapter Two

A Phone Call Recipe
Take equal portions of the sequenced-digit ingredients and add to phone keypad in order as listed.
After pressing the talk button, place phone to ear to complete the call.
Recipe Tip: Do not allow time to cool. Best if the number is called right away and served with a generous scoop of optimism.

One month had silently passed with Aiden watching her unresponsive phone. The hope of Fisher calling began to lose all flavor, and the disappointment had grown too bitter for her taste.

The phone wasn't the only thing to grow quiet. The power tools had completed their tasks of creating the thorn in her side next door, and moved on to torture some other poor victim.

Aiden peered out the front window after closing, glaring at the unwelcome neighbor. "The owners must be into mystery and suspense with hiding the sign under a tarp." The blue covering was held securely in the vines of several bungee cords. "I gotta good mind to sneak up there tonight and uncover it already. It's so silly."

"Just leave it be. Let the owners have their fun with the big reveal," Nora muttered from where she was perched on a stool at the counter, flipping through a new cookbook.

Oddly, neither one of the young women was ever in a rush to leave the café after closing, finding the space more like home than their separate apartments. Aiden glared out the window one last time before heading over to the counter. She placed her head on the countertop and allowed the coolness of the surface and the lingering scent of the orange-scented cleaner to soothe her rattled nerves.

"How were our sales for April?" Nora asked, fastening a tab on a page of the cookbook before looking over.

Aiden kept her head resting on the counter and answered, "Actually better than last year by five percent." Aiden handled all of the financial aspects of the business.

"So why are you worrying about a little competition?"

The frustrated redhead couldn't stifle the eye roll. "It's not open yet."

Nora shrugged her shoulder dismissively. "The paper stated our mystery neighbor will only be serving lunch and dinner. We're a breakfast and lunch café, so surely it won't make much of a difference."

"Our lunch rush will be significantly affected, Nora. Be realistic. Shiny new always draws people's attention. May's sales figures are going to take a nosedive even with tourist season ramping up." Aiden lifted her head and let out a pensive sigh.

"He still hasn't called?" Nora spoke the question softly.

"No. Guess he just wanted to butter me up for a recipe of all things. *Wooed* for a recipe. How pathetic?" She shook her head and rose from the stool to tackle the grocery order for next week. The café used locally sourced ingredients, so weekly orders were a must for freshness.

"He said he would be moving himself and his family business. I'm sure that's kept him quite busy."

"Sure," Aiden muttered with hopes of appeasing Nora enough to drop it. "I've got to get the order put in."

"Please add red endive to the order. I have a new recipe I'd like to try out."

Aiden exhaled, relieved they were back to the safer, less uncomfortable subject of food. One impressive quality Nora possessed was she never pushed people too far. She knew the radio silence from Fisher hurt Aiden's feelings and gave her friend the opportunity to vent. When Aiden didn't seem inclined to do so, she dropped it and moved on.

A week later, just as Aiden locked the front door, her phone alerted her of a new text message. She ignored it for a moment while watching the celebratory group gathering on the sidewalk. Today was the big reveal and grand opening of the mystery restaurant. After being caught spying by one of her own patrons mingling in the crowd, Aiden turned away and pulled the phone from her pocket. She halted midstride at the unexpected message from an unknown number.

Finally a Floridian. Think we could get together soon?

She studied the screen in confusion a few beats before it dawned on her. The sour mood produced by the circus from just outside was pushed away as the smile stretched across her face.

Her fingers were about to reply when the phone disappeared from her hand.

"Don't you dare."

She looked over and found Nora's green eyes giving her a stern look.

"Why not? Look, he included a sunshine emoji. Ain't that so cute?" She pointed it out on the screen.

Nora blinked several times before squinting at her. "Come on, girl. You don't text a guy back right away and give him the satisfaction of knowing you've been desperately waiting for him."

"Nora Bailey, since when do you approve of playing games with men?"

"No games. It's called having a little self-respect." She passed the phone back to Aiden, but didn't let go right away. "I've had to put up with you moping for over a month. It'll be healthy to let him wait at least a day."

Nora was right, as always, so Aiden pocketed the phone. "Let's get out of here."

"What's our plan?" Nora asked as a few more people brushed past them.

"To go over to the sweet shop for an afternoon treat. It's the best location to catch the grand opening without being seen by the crowd." Aiden couldn't figure out how to set her pride to the side long enough to be part of the welcoming wagon for her new competition.

Nora looked at her watch. "Let's go."

The women headed over to the sweet shop and after ordering caramel brownies and coffees, they settled in at a small table by the front window to get a good view.

"Ain't they hospitable," Aiden muttered around a mouthful of fudgy goodness while leaning toward the glass to get a better glimpse. A table laden with refreshments was set up near the alley that separated the two restaurants.

"It's a nice touch for them to be giving out little goody bags and cups of lemonade. I wonder if it's freshly squeezed." Nora took a sip of her coffee.

"Oh, the owner brought me a goody bag earlier. Such a nice guy."

Both Nora and Aiden glanced over to the counter girl. She seemed to take that as her cue to share further. "There's a coupon and sample menu for the restaurant. And a key lime cookie."

"Humph." Before Aiden could ask to see the menu, the crowd began to part as though Moses himself had waved his staff.

Three men began to walk to the front of the

restaurant, one tall and tanned, one with short dreadlocks and dark skin, and one with salt-and-pepper hair, all three in suits even though the sun was dialing up some substantially hot temperatures. Their gazes focused upwards as the tarp was finally removed to reveal a sign crafted out of black metal, turquoise and dark-blue waves etched out around the word *Fishermen's Cove*, giving it a three dimensional effect.

"Now that's one sharp sign," Nora commented.

Moments later, the tall tanned male was handed an oversized pair of scissors. He glanced over his shoulder quickly before slicing through the ribbon fastened to the front door. Aiden was mid-bite when he turned and waved to the applauding group. As the jovial grin lit up his face, the brownie slid from her hand and landed in her coffee. The hot splash dousing her arm did nothing to undo her dismay.

"No way..." Aiden mumbled as Nora inhaled sharply at the same time.

As Phillip Moreau ushered his guests inside the new restaurant, his eyes roamed until landing in Aiden's direction. Surely, he didn't recognize her from that distance, she thought. But somehow he did. He lifted his hand and waved at her, looking relieved, of all things.

"He has a lot of nerve," Nora said.

"What do you mean?" Aiden was once again snagged in Fisher's lure and unable to look away. He nodded his head in the direction of his open entrance, actually inviting her over, but she gave no signal of a reply.

"He was scoping us out that day while saying nothing about his restaurant being built next door." Nora scoffed in disdain before taking another sip of her coffee.

Disappointment seeped in, finally triggering Aiden to shake her head in his direction. She barely made out his dark brows pulling together in maybe his own disappointment before he disappeared inside.

Chapter Three

Recipe for Shock
Begin with one substantial portion of expectation. Dump in the serving of absent phone call, before adding one healthy slap of unforeseen reality and a pinch of regret. Combine until clarity is reached.
Recipe Tip: Do not overmix, so that each ingredient can be analyzed while being served with a side of strong reminder.

Sitting alone in the dark café hours after the big reveal of not only the new restaurant but also the dishonesty of that... that *man*, Aiden still could not come to terms with what happened. With her eyes fixed on the text, she slid her finger over it and hit the delete button. A knock pulled her attention to the glass door and caused the hard knot in her stomach to weave tighter.

Fisher stood waving, minus his coat and tie, while that charming smile continued to beam from his deceitful face. She stayed cemented in her spot at a table near the center of the room and stared at him in disbelief.

"How 'bout letting me in." He motioned to the locked door, still not catching on.

She continued to hold her ground.

After a few more beats lugged by, Fisher's head tilted skyward with understanding before looking back at her. "It's not like that. Let me in and I'll explain."

Her *little fire* began to increase into a full-on blaze while staring him down. She felt like a fool, openly flirting with her rival while he sat on his true identity.

Fisher pushed on the door with hopes of finding it unlocked, but it had no more desire to budge than its owner. Admitting defeat, he shoved his hands into the pockets of his dark trousers and turned to leave, but glanced back one last time with a look of longing before stalking off.

~ ⟡ ~ ⟡ ~ ⟡ ~

As a few weeks moved along with the lunch rush dwindling to resemble more of a lunch drag, Aiden's shock wore off and bitterness began to take over. From past experience, she knew the bitterness could take root and begin withering her outlook on life. Luckily, the frustrated woman was headed to just the place to help her deal with it.

With an aromatic cup of coffee in one hand and beach towel in the other, Aiden joined the small group of no more than a few dozen people on the dusky shore. With no walls to hold back their praise, the seaside worship service was another tradition Aunt Donna introduced her to, and like all traditional things from Aunt Donna it had taken root deep inside Aiden's heart. She paused to take in the sun beginning to warm the surface of the teal water in hues of glittering orange and pink. A few guys strummed their guitars as the worship song harmonized with the ocean's melody. Some sang along while others prepared their makeshift pews. By the time Aiden settled her cup on top of the outstretched towel, the song concluded.

"Welcome to another day the Lord has made. Before we get too settled, how about we welcome one another." Their pastor waved his hand out in encouragement.

The guitars picked back up and serenaded the gathering as they began moving around. Aiden stood to greet a friend but stifled a groan when she spotted a new face in the group. Fisher stood tall and proud with a devilish smile on his face. An elderly lady ambled over to him, but he kept his focus on Aiden as he offered the woman a hug. After he was free, he began a path directly to Aiden, but she dodged through the crowd. Hoping by some miracle the tiny group could somehow hide her from the annoyance hot on her heels, Aiden divvied out some welcome hugs.

Fisher graciously spoke to each person he passed, but his goal to catch her seemed to never waver. Aiden continued to shoot warning glares over her shoulder for him to back off. He, in return, widened his grin and accepted her warning as a challenge instead.

Only a few minutes eased by, but it felt like eternity to her, as she helplessly watched Fisher close the distance between them. The two of them were playing some sluggish game of chase, and she knew for certain she was about to lose. After offering Preacher Jeff a quick hug, Aiden turned and plowed right into set of outstretched arms. Before she could flee, Fisher encircled her in his warm embrace, and boy, did she hate how nice it felt.

Pulling her flush against his body, Fisher murmured in her ear, "Tag, you're it." His rich chuckle gave away just how pleased he was with himself.

Not wanting to cause a scene, Aiden whispered harshly, "Let go."

Of course, he ignored her and began speaking at a volume the group would surely be able to hear. "Thank you, my sweet friend. It's good to see you, too. I'd love to sit with you this morning." He leaned back to catch her reaction.

She was stubborn enough to not give him the satisfaction, knowing all eyes were on the town's restaurant rivals. That juicy tidbit of news whispered around quickly. Even an article was published in the local paper, speculating about the two of them not even talking. Nora encouraged Aiden to brush it off and accept the fact that any type of publicity was good publicity, but that was easier said than done.

Realizing the guitar and crowd had hushed, Aiden plastered on a pleasant smile and gestured Fisher toward her towel. She sat down but nearly stood back up when he boldly planted himself firmly by her side, but refrained when realizing several eyes were glued to them. Even before Preacher Jeff began to present the day's message, Aiden was already having to ask for forgiveness for the mean thoughts passing through her head over the infuriating man. Fisher was hogging her personal space, hogging her beach towel, hogging her normal lunch business, and, worst of all, hogging her thoughts.

As the pastor began to speak, everyone's focus shifted toward him, so Aiden took the opportunity to scoot over. Undeterred, Fisher casually scooted over to eliminate the new space between them. Like two juveniles, they began another game with Aiden scooting away, followed by Fisher removing her progress. From the pure happiness broadcasting through his smile and the warmth of his touch, her body betrayed her by not wanting to move away. Before allowing his effects to cause her to do something stupid like hold his hand or sink closer into his side, she scooted once again to break their connection.

Aiden soon ran out of towel real-estate, Fisher boldly clamped his arm around her shoulder and whispered not anywhere close to quietly, "Get still before you disrupt service."

Eyes darted their way, proving his intention of being heard a success. His grin widened, showcasing a set of pearly white teeth, as he shook his head in mock-reprimand. Then, when Aiden felt she couldn't be any more mortified, he pushed his luck even further by coasting his fingertips down her arm before entwining them with her unsuspecting fingers.

She tried to snatch away from his grasp, but he had her hand in a vice grip, daring her to make a scene.

"Let go," she said out of the side of mouth.

Fisher leaned over and placed a kiss on the side of her head and whispered, "Maybe *you* should just let go."

How dare him! Aiden sat rigidly still for the remainder of the service, fuming while trying to figure out a plan to get back at Phillip Moreau for toying with her emotions, deceiving her, and making a mockery of her on that beach.

Sorry, God. It's his fault. Not mine. She glared up at the man she briefly and naively regarded as a sun deity, realizing he was closer in lines to being a spawn of Satan.

Chapter Four

Secret Recipe for Revenge
Begin by dividing aggression into manageable portions.
Add a little at a time to a serving of quick wits and a
heaping amount of valuable information. Mix ingredients
vigorously until the plan comes together.
Recipe Tip: If the proper balance of ingredients isn't used,
the consistency will break and revenge may become poor in
taste.

Aiden practically ran away during closing prayer last Sunday, abandoning her towel and the confusing feelings Fisher stirred up. The sweet group of *gossipers,* she obviously worshiped with each Sunday on the beach, had quickly taken it upon themselves to clear up the misconception that the two restaurateurs were feuding. Those sweet busybodies let it be known about the two getting right cozy with each other. News breezed around that Fisher and Aiden were a couple, how the two held hands during the service, how Fisher had affectionately given Aiden a kiss. Blah, blah, blah.

Aiden kept a tight lip when asked about their couple status, but Fisher seemed to have no trouble adding fuel to the rumor fire. He tossed around that familiar line, *I don't kiss and tell,* and was quick to say how much he was attracted to the *Little Fire.*

She wanted nothing more to do with the manipulative punk, but he had other plans. Each day Fisher would send a text message and each day Aiden would delete it without replying.

Monday – *I really enjoyed sitting with you during service. I'll bring the towel next Sunday.*
Delete.
Tuesday – *I'd love for you to stop by and let me give you a tour after closing.*
Delete.
Wednesday – *You need to give me a chance. We have a connection and you know it.*
Delete.
Thursday – *Won't you just let it go already!*
Delete.

She was just about to delete Friday's message that simply stated, *thinking of you,* when a knock sounded at the back door. Odd, since it was only five in the morning. Realizing Nora must have forgotten her keys, Aiden unlocked the door and opened it wide with eyes still trained on her phone.

"Mornin'" she muttered.

"Mornin'" a deep voice greeted back, causing the phone to fly from her hand and a screech to peal from her mouth.

She was already grabbing a broom, when the vaguely familiar man threw his hands up in defense.

30

"Whoa, cher. I'm just trying to deliver an order of fish."

It was then that she realized the stranger before her with the neat dreadlocks was one of the suits from Fisher's grand opening. When she finally lowered the broom, he offered his hand. "Levi Mitchel. I'm Fisher's boat captain."

Reluctantly, she took his hand and muttered, "Aiden." She caught sight of Nora coming through the door. Her friend's eyes went wide. Aiden released his hand and gestured behind him. "This is my business partner, Nora."

The man offered her friend a much wider smile along with his hand. "Very nice to meet you. I'm Levi."

Aiden was taken aback when she caught Nora actually batting her eyelashes at the man. "You said something about fish?" she asked, breaking into their little moment.

"Ah yeah." He stepped back outside and lugged in a cooler bag. "Freshly caught this mornin'. Fisher said this is a gift, so no charge."

Aiden eyed the bag and folded her arms. "Let me guess, Mahi-Mahi."

"Dat it is."

"I love your accent," Nora said in a soft tone Aiden had never heard before.

"New Orleans. And you have one yourself," Levi commented, flirt filling his tone.

"Good grief," Aiden said rather loudly before yanking the bag from his hand, emptying the contents onto the counter, and handing it back to him.

"Any message you'd like me to relay to my man for the fish?"

"Tell him I still hate him," she deadpanned.

Levi roared in a hearty laugh. "Gotcha. Nora, it was a pleasure." He tipped his head in her direction and he sauntered out the door.

Once the door was shut, Nora went to inspect the fish. "That's some beautiful fish. I can look up a few recipes once we get the morning rush settled down."

Staring at the pale-pink fish in the clear bags, a devious idea bloomed in Aiden's thoughts. Her lips curled as she snatched one of the bags. "I've got another idea for this pack. You can take the rest of it home and share with your grandma." She hustled outside and hid the bag on the back of the deck before returning to the kitchen.

"That's so wasteful," Nora scolded while tying the apron around her tiny waist.

"It has a purpose. No worries." Aiden brushed off her friend's pointed look, and headed to the coffeepots to get them started up.

Shortly after breakfast, Aiden's phone alerted a new text message.

Saturday – *Hope you enjoyed the fish.*

The text was accompanied by a winking emoji. "Oh I'm gonna enjoy it, all right," she muttered while hitting the delete button.

Another message showed up by the end of the weekend.

Sunday – *I missed you at the worship service. Some*

old lady forgot her towel, so I let her have your spot. Just wasn't the same...

Delete.

Aiden went back and forth until it was too late to go to the service. She knew she was being a coward, but Fisher couldn't be trusted any more than she could trust her resolve to keep resisting him. When the man was before her, every emotion and thought and reaction became clouded over by his mere presence.

As she settled into bed that night, another message taunted her.

Late Sunday – *What's with this runaway bride stuff?*

DELETE!

Aiden wished she could delete the embarrassment as easily, but that deeply embedded thorn was still causing her soreness six years later. She figured someone took it upon themselves to fill him in on her broken engagement. *Lovely.*

Monday's text never showed up, so Aiden suspected Fisher had finally found out her little surprise. It was obvious since her lunch rush was back in full force and the murmurings sweeping through the crowded tables about the reeking problem at Fishermen's Cove.

Tuesday – *The fish was a gift. Why did you have to go and make a stink out of it?*

Aiden had just locked the door for the day when she finally had a chance to read the message on her phone due to the day being slammed. A laugh slipped out, knowing the man had to be irate at finding the rotting fish in his potted shrubberies at the main entrance, but he still somehow managed to crack a joke about it. She was pretty proud of the stunt she successfully pulled off. The after-midnight stroll Friday night to give him the fish back went off without a hitch.

Her finger hovered over the delete button, but she couldn't resist answering this one.

Aiden – *A gift? Not hardly. That's you trying to ease a guilty conscience for stealing my recipe.*

As soon as she hit send, the little bubble popped up to indicate he was typing. She frowned at the screen before pocketing the phone and worked on switching the lights off, not caring for whatever excuse he could come up with for having the recipe featured on his menu. She knew this because she and Nora had crept the restaurant's Facebook page and discovered the menu. As she made it to the small office to write out the deposit, her phone pinged. Taking a deep breath, she read the message.

Fisher – *You willingly gave it to me. And your number.*

Annoyed by the truth of his words, Aiden deleted it with wishes she could delete the whole mess the man had made in her perfectly content life.

The afternoon silently tiptoed by with Aiden making a trip to the bank and running a few errands, but her mind refused to give her a break. Unable to focus on anything else, she ended up back at the café and spent the evening in a lounge chair on the back patio, hoping the ocean would emit its calming effect on her.

As the darkness of nightfall completely erased the day's light, Aiden listened to the sea breeze mingle with the lively sounds of the neighboring restaurant. She slid her attention toward his back deck and noticed the potted shrubberies that had been moved there from the front entrance. With a wry smile, she refocused on the glowing waves until drifting off to sleep.

A door banging shut roused her later on in the night. Looking over, she noticed several wait staff heading out, followed by the kitchen staff and chef shortly after.

As Aiden stood to stretch, she realized a few lights were still shining from Fishermen's Cove. Curiosity propelled her forward and the next thing she knew, her feet had come to a halt at the back entrance. Reaching out, she found it unlocked. Not stopping there, she let herself in. The kitchen was set up close to hers but on a bigger scale. The entire place was at least twice the size as the café, but that didn't bother her. What bothered her was when she entered the dining area, the sign over the front entrance caught her attention.

Fisher edged into her peripheral, but she kept her eyes focused on the words scrolling over the teak wood planks. *I will make you fishers of men.*

"I see you stole this idea from me as well." She pointed to the sign.

"I've stolen *nothing* from you. The sign was actually ordered before I met you. I can pull the invoice for verification." There was a clear edge of annoyance to his voice.

Aiden brushed past him and wandered around the space. Although it was new construction, the restaurant easily conveyed a cozy warmth normally achieved only after a long length of time. Wide-planked floors, looking as old as the Ark, creaked with charm underneath her feet and led her over to the hefty driftwood bar. As she studied the large photos hanging behind it, Fisher's presence drew close behind her. It was on the tip of her tongue to ask him about the images depicting various days on the open sea, but her mouth clamped down with stubbornness. Casual conversation with that man would probably only get her into trouble.

She continued to peruse the space, appreciating how the creamy blue walls gave the illusion of being faded by time. If she didn't hate the idea of the place so much, she would be in love with its ambiance.

Clearing his throat, Fisher finally asked, "Does this visit have a purpose?"

Aiden turned and choked on the condescending retort about to push past her lips when realizing he'd moved to stand right behind her. It nearly knocked the unprepared woman on her backside the moment those golden eyes locked with hers.

She slowly blinked and looked away. "You did a nice job with the design and details." She waved a hand around, deciding she really wasn't up for a round of sparring with him.

Fisher took a step back and crossed his arms over

his broad chest, causing the light-blue button-down to strain against his biceps. The snort he released sounded nowhere close to amusement.

Aiden turned away from the temptation of being friendly to him, knowing he was probably mad... no, downright livid would be a better description. Her little stunt did cost him profit for a few days. She should apologize. *Should* being the keyword and she gave it her all to ignore it.

Sea glass adorning the back of driftwood shelves caught her eye. They were alluring and whimsical— two words that described the owner to a T. She found him in everything lately, even though she hardly knew him.

Aiden sidled over to the hostess stand, made up of wooden fishing crates, and helped herself to a menu. It was filled with succulent offerings, many with a Cajun flare. The descriptions had her mouth watering until her eyes landed on one dish that would forever put a sour taste in her mouth.

"I can't believe you have this stolen dish on your menu." It took all her might to not knock him in the head with the leather menu.

Fisher hastily ran his fingers through his wavy locks. "It's not considered stolen when someone *gives* it to you." He huffed while shaking his head. "I made so many changes, it's nothing like your dish now. So it's time you let it go."

Let go. Let it go. That seemed to be his ever-present advice. But Aiden was tenacious to a fault and had no desire to *let it go.*

Releasing a heavy sigh, Fisher grasped her hand. "Come on. I'll show you."

Aiden tugged to free her hand, but the effort did little good. "Show me what?"

"The recipe."

She yanked once more and this time he actually relented. "You know how to cook?"

"Yes, but I mostly leave that to my chef while I run the front of the house." He offered his hand this time instead of taking hers without permission. Of course she crossed her arms and refused. Giving up, Fisher made his way to the kitchen. "You coming or not?"

Aiden stared at his backside in those tailored navy trousers as he retreated into the kitchen, torn between stubbornness and curiosity. Nobody ever accused her of lacking in either one of those characteristic departments. She just couldn't walk away. Brushing off the stubbornness, curiosity forced her to go find out what that man was up to. She found him gathering ingredients from the industrial-sized refrigerator.

"I knew you wouldn't be able to resist." He turned around with an armful of citrus, peppers, and spices with a slight smile on his face.

After placing the items on the work table, Fisher untucked his shirt, rolled up the sleeves, and released a few top buttons. Aiden couldn't look away, and his sullen demeanor made her gravitate closer to his side. Something about a brooding Fisher was sort of sexy in her opinion. Once he produced a knife and bowl and set out to slicing and dicing the ingredients with impeccable knife skills, Aiden's attention moved to him preparing the salsa. The only sound was the knife tapping against the butcher block, so when he finally spoke, it startled her.

"We took out the mint and spiced it up with cilantro and jalapeno peppers. Also took out the grapefruit and added plum tomatoes."

"You're pretty good with that knife," she complimented before stopping herself.

Fisher shrugged as he made quick work of finely dicing a red onion. "I've filleted so many fish, a knife just seems like an extension of my hand anymore."

He placed all of the diced ingredients in a bowl and drizzled it with olive oil before finishing it off with salt and pepper. Gripping the bowl in one hand, he expertly tossed it all together with a simple flick of his wrist. He grabbed a clean spoon and scooped up some of the salsa, and turned toward Aiden to offer her a taste.

Reluctant to allow him to feed her, she hesitated until he lifted a dark eyebrow in challenge. She opened her mouth and accepted the bite. As soon as she began to chew, the spicy notes of jalapeno woke her palette and before she could hold it back, she moaned an, "Hmm..."

Fisher's smile finally made it to his golden eyes. He swiped a bite of his own before placing the salsa in a container and fastening a lid over it. "I made this for you. It pairs perfectly with fresh Mahi-Mahi." He handed it to her and began cleaning up his mess, but there was no missing the little bit of frustration laced into that last sentence.

Aiden stood there holding the bowl as he cleaned, not sure if he had just dismissed her or not. Either way, she wasn't ready to go, so she stayed silently in her spot by the table and quietly observed his broad shoulders working the fabric of the blue shirt while he washed the few dishes.

Fisher shut the water off and turned around while drying his hands on a cloth. Tossing it behind him, he crossed his arms and leaned against the edge of the stainless steel sink in a confident stance while watching Aiden.

"You should just go ahead and admit that you're crazy about me, so we can move on. We were meant to be friends not enemies. And I bet if you give us a chance, this friendship could turn into something much more." He sounded so sure of himself. "From the moment I saw you, it's what I've wanted."

"Friendships can't be formed on a foundation of lies." Her words wiped the smile off his face.

"I didn't lie to you." Fisher rubbed the dark stubble along his chin.

"Lie of omission is the same thing. You introduced yourself under false pretenses. A fisherman and not the owner of my neighboring rival."

"I didn't do it out of malice or anything. We hit it off so easy and then you said you were the owner... I just wanted to get to know you without this getting in the way." He gestured around the kitchen. "I wanted you to see me as Fisher and not your rival. Besides, I am a fisherman. Always will be."

"I don't like deceit and dishonesty and have already dealt with enough of that in my past to last a lifetime."

Fisher pushed off the sink and moved to stand uncomfortably close in front of her. Leaning down, he angled his head until she gave in and met his gaze. "Please believe it was never my intention hurt you. I thought I'd come here and surprise you and we'd laugh it off. I didn't plan for it to turn out this way. I truly am sorry." He took the bowl from her hand, placed it back on the table, and pulled her in for a hug.

Aiden steeled herself and kept her hands by her side, refusing to return the embrace. "But we still don't agree."

Fisher released a heavy sigh against her neck, making her shudder. "How about an impasse?" His words caressed her neck in the same spot as the sigh and it was all she could do to not give in to the indulgence of being in his arms.

Shivering, she wiggled out of his arms and headed for the door. "I need to go…"

He stretched an arm out to block the exit and handed over the forgotten bowl of salsa. "At least think about it." A hint of defeat entered his expression as he stepped back and allowed her to walk out.

Chapter Five

Impasse Recipe
Take equal portions of both sides and mix in the realization that the differences of opinions won't come together at first... or maybe never. Allow the situation to marinate over a period of time until an agreement is met.
Recipe Tip: Best if this recipe is not rushed. If one side of the argument takes hasty action, the other side will sour with resentment and the entire recipe will be ruined.

Aiden stayed up way too late replaying Fisher's words and the way he held her with such ease. With less than three hours' worth of sleep, she listened to the voicemail while standing in the middle of the café's abandoned kitchen with trepidation. There was no doubting the day would surely be a long one.

"Hey. Grandma had another spell. I'm at the hospital with her, so switch out the regular menus with the simpler ones and try not to burn anything." Nora's voice sounded tired, but her bossiness was present as always.

Aiden sent her a quick message, *call me if you need me*, before pocketing the phone. She tied on an apron for the day as she whispered a prayer for Nora and her grandmother. Her friend was sort of in the same boat as her, with Nora's parents in Jamaica, leaving the responsibility of caring for her grandmother resting solely on her petite shoulders.

It turned out to be one hectic day, even with the simple menus, but Aiden wasn't complaining. It meant business was getting closer to being back to normal. There was finally a lull in the orders around closing time, so she took the opportunity to go check on the front of the house. Patrons filled most of the tables while smiling waitresses attentively met their dining needs.

Aiden was about to retreat back into the kitchen when a teal flyer caught her attention. She took a good look around and found each tabletop dotted with the blue papers.

"What's with this?" Aiden grabbed the paper from the counter and waved it around for answers.

Brittany looked up from refilling a customer's glass with water. "Oh. Fisher brought those by. He's having a live band Saturday night. He asked if we'd help spread the word." The blonde beamed, thinking she did something good.

Was last night just another game he was playing? Aiden started seeing red as she looked down at the blue paper. If that sucker wanted her help with drumming up business, she would surely oblige. It only took until closing before she figured out just how to go about doing that.

The idea materialized just as she was filling out her weekly ad for the local paper. She had waited until the last minute, but the ads lady was always accommodating, even though the paper went out the following morning.

"So just the regular ad this week?" Becky asked.

Aiden moved the phone to her left ear and pulled up last week's ad on her computer. "Sure, just take out the coupon."

"No problem. Anything else?"

As Aiden's eyes studied the little coupon for buy one entrée, get one half price, it hit her. "Actually there is. My friend Phillip Moreau needs an ad, and I almost forgot he asked me to handle it for him since I was calling you anyway."

"Aww. That's so sweet of you. Is it true the two of you are secretly engaged?"

Aiden refrained the snort begging to dispute the rumor, but rolled her eyes at the computer instead. "We don't kiss and tell," she said on a silly giggle, going for effect.

Becky joined in with the laugh, not knowing she was part of the joke. "Okay, so what does he need in the ad?"

She glanced over at the blue flyer. "Just that Fishermen's Cove is having a live band Saturday evening... and... put a coupon for free appetizers and tea." She hastily thought it over and added, "No purchase necessary."

"Wow. That's very generous of him." Becky's keyboard tapped out at a rapid-fire pace in the background.

He just doesn't know how generous.

"It's sure to draw a crowd."

The keyboard tempo paused. "Let's see... I actually have a cancellation for a half page ad, or if he wants smaller there's an eighth page available. Those two are the only ones available for this week."

Aiden thought it over and the small one wouldn't draw enough eyes, but that half page was going to be a costly way to get back at the jerk. Squeezing her eyes shut to avoid seeing the silliness of her ways, she blurted, "He said go big."

"The big ad is also on a color page. You know that's going to cost extra, right?"

Aiden grimaced, knowing Nora would surely kill her for the expense. "How much?"

"It regularly costs six-fifty, but beings that it's his first ad with us, I can do it for five hundred."

Aiden swallowed hard and muttered, "Okay."

"Great. I already have his information around here somewhere, so I'll contact Mr. Moreau this afternoon to let him know about the bill."

Aiden sat up straighter in her desk chair. "No!" She caught her tone and softened it before continuing. "I'd like to purchase his first ad with the paper as a surprise welcome gift." She let out a breath. The satisfaction would have been sweeter if he had to pay for the ad himself, but she had no other choice. Otherwise, he would discover what she had done and fix it.

"You're in love. Don't dare deny it. I can't wait to see the engagement announcement in the paper. I'll even do that one on the house!"

Aiden's eyes rolled again. Were people that

desperate to see her married off? She brushed her annoyance away and decided to allow Becky to live in her false assumption.

"Just email me the invoice and I'll get it paid within the hour." *Before Nora finds out and cancels it.*

"Okay. You'll have it in a few."

"Thanks, Becky."

"No problem!"

After the phone call ended, Aiden worked on the deposit and waited for the invoice to arrive. She wanted to get it paid and put the prank behind her, knowing it was right stupid and immature.

How about an impasse? Fisher's words whispered around the office. This time as she remembered them, Aiden allowed a very unladylike snort to have its moment. *Impasse.* He apparently had no clue as to what that word meant. Or most likely, he knew exactly what he was doing.

Wednesday – *I'm sneaking out of here by 7. Let me grill you some Mahi-Mahi for a late supper?*
Delete.
Thursday – *Why you gotta be so blame stubborn!*
Delete.
Friday – *Hope you come over to check out the band tomorrow night.*
Delete.
Saturday – *I want to see you later. Please.*
Delete.

Aiden put her phone away as they began closing

shop on Saturday, knowing he would change his mind real quick-like as soon as those coupons began piling up later. She was kind enough to snip coupons from several papers and distribute them right along with the Saturday brunch orders. And Saturday brunch at the café always brought in a sizable crowd. One of the errant, little slips of paper peeked from underneath a table. Aiden bent to pick it up, when she heard Nora tsk from behind her.

"Why are you helping that man all of a sudden?" All sorts of accusation mingled with the question.

Aiden whirled around and caught sight of Nora standing unusually tall for a short person, with her arms crossed and eyes narrowed.

"Why can't I help someone out?" She lashed her own question out instead of answering.

"I know you better than that. Gwaan?" Nora's stare bored right through her, making the redhead fidget.

For heaven's sake... Here we go with the Jamaican jargon. "Nothing's going on!" Aiden threw her hands in the air and marched towards the kitchen.

"I hope you're right."

"Why's it matter so much to you?" She began unloading the dishwasher.

Nora hopped up on the counter and swing her legs back and forth. "Because Grandma is on the mends, so I have a date tonight. I don't want any of your shenanigans to get in the way of it."

"Why would anything I do get in the—" That's when it hit her. She froze with hands gripping a plate

47

in each. "You're going out with Levi?"

"What's the harm in that?"

"Because he's the enemy!" Aiden's arms flapped in the air with the plates waving around with craziness, looking like a deranged lunatic. Well, that's what Nora said...

After calling Aiden a lunatic, Nora backed off. Before she left for the day, the petite woman poked her head cautiously into the office to find Aiden staring at a blank computer screen.

Clearing her throat, Nora confessed, "I'll be next door tonight."

The door smacked shut before Aiden could twirl around in the desk chair. "Next door?" she hollered. "Really?" After no answer was delivered, she slumped into her cushiony chair, feeling rather uncomfortable.

Sunday morning arrived with the sun brimming over in exuberance for another day, yet Aiden was knotted up with reluctance. She tossed and turned last night, knowing she foolishly toyed with Fisher's profits with the little stunt with the coupon. The blankets offered no comforting shelter even though she burrowed in them until making herself late for worship service on the beach.

Tossing on a thin hoodie and a pair of shorts, she grabbed her bike and made the short trek down the road to the café. Too much of a coward to join the group on the beach, she hid in the shadows of the café's back deck. Luckily, Pastor Jeff's voice carried gracefully with aid of the ocean breeze so she could hear him just fine from the hiding spot. As he read over some announcements, Aiden's eyes betrayed her by scoping out the small gathering.

Fisher... The man was too easy to spot—hat turned backwards so that the gentle wind played with the wayward curls sneaking out from around the edges, a plain white T-shirt looking nowhere near plain, frayed cargo shorts with the blue hue severely faded. He sat on *her* towel, leaving a spot on it towards his left vacant. He leaned over and whispered something to his friend Levi, who was sitting on his own beach towel, causing his buddy to punch him playfully in the arm. Fisher was such a lively creature, gesturing his hands animatedly as he told Levi about something that had the poor guy's shoulder's vibrating from holding back the desire to laugh.

The two guys settled down after this and focused forward on the sermon, but every so often Fisher would scan around as though he was looking for someone in particular. And Aiden hated to admit she wanted it to be her who he was hoping to see.

The sermon concentrated on forgiveness, making a fine sheen of perspiration break out along her skin. *Way to kick me when I'm down, Big Guy!* Aiden lifted her eyes to heaven with reproach. She knew she was to blame and not Him, but it always felt better to point the guilt in another direction.

As the closing song concluded, the group began to stand and meander on with their respective day's plans. Aiden scooted from the shadows and headed for cover. Before she made any progress, a warm hand grasped her upper arm and anchored her by the back door. She knew who the hand belonged to and found no satisfaction in being so aware of him.

"I shelled out over two hundred *free* appetizers last night and double that in glasses of tea."

"Oh." Aiden cringed, hoping the number wouldn't be *that* high. She refused to turn around and face what she had done.

Fisher surprised her by leaning in and nipping the edge of her ear with his teeth. "Yep. Crazy how that happened." He moved closer and gripped her hips, causing her shoulders to meet his firm chest. "Beings that I didn't place any ad to my recollection. You wouldn't know who the guilty party responsible for that would be, do ya?"

Her heartrate quickened and breathing became a chore. A strange yet intoxicating mix of fear and desire kept Aiden uncharacteristically quiet as this infuriating man made out with the side of her neck while building his case against her.

"No? Well, if you happen to find out, how 'bout tell the culprit I owe her a big thank you. My profit doubled last night." He nipped her neck once more before relinquishing his grasp. "You should have come by and had a free appetizer and tea with Nora. She's great." He threw this last tidbit out over his shoulder as he bounced down the deck stairs.

Before Aiden could find her voice to sass or beg him not to leave, Fisher had disappeared down the small alley between their buildings. Slumping against the door, she managed to drag in several staggering breaths. The man was going to drive her crazy, if she couldn't figure out how to deal with him and her bizarre feelings for him.

I dislike him.

But, I sort of like him...

No, I really do loathe him.

I lust him...

What? No!

Shaking her head as to rebuke the thought, Aiden stormed inside the café and away from the wayward feelings Phillip Moreau just helped to scatter all over the place.

Chapter Six

Guilty Recipe
Begin with one unhealthy scoop of resentment. Add in several dashes of errant opinions on how to seek justice and mix with various steps on fulfilling the spiteful act. Let stew until it all goes too far.
Recipe Tip: Warning. Once this recipe is complete, consequences normally follow.

"You're peculiar relationship with that man is becoming costly," Nora scolded while eyeing Aiden's latest purchase propped against the kitchen wall.

"I'm righting a wrong, and then I'm washing my hands of him and this entire fiasco," Aiden promised.

It had taken over a week to track down the five-foot-tall framed artwork. It had also been a silent week from Fisher. He was even a no-show for the worship service, but Nora let it slip about him going on a fishing trip with Levi. Aiden tried not to be disappointed by his sudden silence. *Maybe he's still mad at me.*

The latest rumor flickered through her thoughts, making her think it was probably a good idea he hadn't been around. Aiden smoothed the fitted shirt along her flat abdomen and shuddered at the outlandish thought. She made the mistake of wearing a frumpy dress to work due to not being in the mood to do laundry. And that's all it took to start the fictitious story of her being pregnant with Fisher's baby. Since then, she'd made it a point to wear fitted clothing that showed no evidence of a baby bump.

"He'll love this." Nora ran her fingertips over the beveled surface of the sea glass, recapturing Aiden's wandering attention. The frame was made up of frosted teals, indigos, aqua-blues, and bleached whites that swirled together in an ocean wave pattern.

"The frame or the canvas?" Aiden asked as she attached the apology card using a decorative fishnet.

"Definitely both. It's very thoughtful of you to find one with The Fisherman's Prayer."

Aiden finished securing the card and took a step back to read the words.

I pray that I may live to fish
Until my dying day.
And when it comes to my last cast,
I then most humbly pray:
When in the Lord's great landing net
And peacefully asleep
That in His mercy I be judged
Big enough to keep.

From the look Nora was giving her, Aiden knew her friend was reading way too much into this. "Stop looking at me like that!" She grabbed up the bulky gift and marched it out the back and over to Fisher's backdoor where she left it leaning against the doorframe.

Aiden felt the guilt of her actions alleviate as she stepped back onto her own deck. The sun caught her eye, so she paused to pay it some respect and to whisper a prayer of thanks for another day. Inhaling the briny air, she watched the sunrays kiss the top of the ocean, bathing the teal water in hues of pink and orange. The smile crept on her face and refused to let anything wipe it away. Early morning was hands down her favorite part of the day—a fresh start with optimism on the horizon. Feeling energized and eager to face another busy summer day, she left the majestic view of the Gulf Coast and headed back inside.

Morning moped around at a sluggish pace, but Aiden refused to allow her smile to falter. She easily shared it with the very few elderly couples who came in to dine. She even sat down with one little lady and chatted her up as they both enjoyed a cup of coffee.

By eleven o'clock the smile began to slip, but she kept pulling it back up into place. She reluctantly sent the two morning helpers home early and was now gazing awkwardly at the abandoned dining area.

"This is what you get for monkeying around with Fisher's business." Nora's accent laced her scold, revealing her frustration. She hardly pronounced any of the words' endings.

Aiden went on the defense. "That has nothing to do with this." Her hands gestured around the café ghost town.

"Dawg nyam yu suppa." Nora muttered, sounding a lot like her grandma in Aiden's ears.

"Lands sake, woman, I gave him an apology gift. This is not some consequence for my coupon stunt."

Wanting no more of Nora's proverbs, Aiden busied herself with dumping the full pots of thickening coffee. Nora joined her in the kitchen but said nothing more. Aiden still felt the need to make up an excuse for their poor business morning that looked to be trickling into the lunch hour as well.

Focused on scrubbing the tarred residue from the bottom of the pots, she said, "Some place in town must be running a breakfast special."

Nora kept voicing her grumbles as lunch showed up in the same mournful procession as the morning, and Aiden kept brushing it off. After dismissing the lunch help around one, Nora planted herself at the counter with her laptop to scope out new recipes.

"Why don't you go to our Facebook page and post a lunch special for tomorrow," Aiden suggested as she moved over to lock the front door two hours earlier than normal.

"Yah. That's a good idea. Maybe we can get rid of your lousy mojo."

Aiden was about to sass back, but the words were lost when she spotted a line forming on the sidewalk. "How peculiar," she mumbled, craning her neck to get a better view of next door.

"What was that?" Nora asked.

"Something's going on at Fishermen's Cove..." Before she could elaborate, something else quite fishy caught her attention.

People passing by kept gawking at something on the front of the café. They would pause, shrug their shoulders, and direct their path next door to join the growing line. Before Aiden could unlock the door to see what the commotion was about, Nora spoke up.

"Dawg nyam yu suppa." She tsked. "You getting them consequences."

Aiden whirled around. "What are you yammering on about?"

Nora smoothed her already smooth hair and pointed to the laptop screen displaying the café's FB page. "We've been hacked." Aiden rushed over as Nora began to read the pinned post. *"Due to personal issues, The Orange Blossom Café will be closed Tuesday, June 21st. Fishermen's Cove, located just next door, will gladly accept the expired coupons for a free appetizer and tea as a consolation. Check with the newspaper for back issues. To see this week's specials, go to Fishermen's Cove homepage. Link below."*

"That man is asking for it!" Aiden shouted as she jerked the door open to see what other gift he'd left her.

Her stomach knotted as the enormous vinyl banner caught her attention immediately with its bright-orange border. It contrasted nicely against the creamy grey siding of the café, sure to draw eyes. The words, displayed in a teal hue, advertised the same declaration as the café's FB page. She was obviously not the only one willing to spend a little money on this runaway train of sabotage.

Ignoring the whispers from behind her, Aiden ripped the banner down and flung it in Fisher's alley trashcan. It didn't quite make it inside, instead, the banner dressed the trashcan like a vividly colored sash. She glared at it before hightailing it back inside, where she found Nora rummaging around in the paper recycling bin.

"What are you doing?"

Nora unearthed two coupons and fanned them in air and marched toward the exit. "Let's go."

Aiden didn't return her friend's enthusiasm, but gravely followed to join the line outside. A few patrons did a double-take when they spotted the café's owners waiting along with them. Aiden tried conjuring up a smile that ended up resembling closer to a grimace. She exhaled the breath she was holding when Nora moved a little in front of her in a protective manner, even though she was a few inches shorter.

Nora snorted and motioned towards the banner in the alley. "A big joke. These two," she started and pointed over her shoulder at Aiden and then to Fisher, who just happened to pop his head out the front entrance in perfect timing, "are such tricksters. Mr. Moreau is actually treating Aiden and me to lunch to make up for his latest prank."

Fisher looked at her with an eyebrow raised. "I am?"

"Absolutely. You also promised us a reserved table with no wait. Such a gentlemanly offer." Nora smiled sweetly, her green eyes sparkling.

Aiden couldn't recall ever seeing her friend looking more wicked than in that very moment, and she inwardly cheered over her bold spunk. With his cocky smirk faltering, Fisher must have picked up on it as well. Running his right hand through his golden-brown locks, he beckoned them forward with his left. Nora laced her hand with Aiden's and began walking proudly to the entrance.

One thing Aiden could always count on was Phillip Moreau never let an opportunity pass to ruffle her feathers. He deliberately stepped in her way so that Aiden had no choice but to brush against him as she passed by. The ultra-soft fabric of his white linen shirt was almost her undoing, but she reined it in and kept walking. She cut him a glare with him returning it with that mischievous smirk those pouty lips favored. Fisher placed his hand on the small of her back and led them to the hostess stand where he spoke softly to the young brunette. It was obvious he wanted to avoid a scene.

"Alexa, I need the next available two-top for these ladies." He glanced at them, as both women took in the jam-packed dining area.

Aiden's surprised gaze landed on her apology gift. The framed canvas was already displayed on the right wall, just above a vacant four-top table. "Actually, we want to sit by that lovely artwork." She pointed.

"Umm... We're a bit busy, cher, and need all available chairs." Those caramel eyes watched her guardedly, almost begging for a brief reprieve.

Aiden's hands hitched onto her hips as her eyes narrowed, having no desire to grant him any sort of reprieve. "You wouldn't have that problem if you hadn't flat-out lied about the café being closed today." She received her desired effect when several widened eyes shot in their direction and Fisher actually flinched in response.

Good. He should feel guilty, she thought with smug satisfaction.

His ample lips pressed into a hard line as Fisher ushered them to the four-top table, and like a gentleman, pulled both women's chairs out for them. After grabbing menus and placing them before Nora and Aiden, he knelt by the table.

"Order whatever you want... Stay as long as you want... Just please be nice... Please." His tone was pleading as he offered a tense smile.

Aiden wanted to pester Fisher and not be nice at all, but his crisp cologne and the warmth of his body overwhelmed her. Then he reached his hand out and placed it on her knee, gentle and kind, he looked up at her. Barely able to swallow, she nodded her head lamely.

He let out a sigh and gave her knee an appreciative squeeze before standing. "I'll give you ladies a few minutes to look over the menu."

Aiden watched him saunter off into the bustling crowd, hearing a raucous snort. She turned her attention back to Nora. "What's with you today? Are you trying to hit a snort count goal or something?"

Nora rolled those emerald eyes. "You two acting

like school kids, showing your attraction for one another by being ugly." She snickered for a change of sound.

"What?"

"You know how the boy pulls the girl's pigtails and pushes her down, instead of admitting he likes her."

Before Aiden could rebuke the claim, a waiter sidled up to the table with an overflowing basket of conch fritters and tall glasses of tea.

"Hello, ladies. I'm Kaden. Fisher said for me to start you with this and to take very good care of you." The young man grinned and winked at Aiden as if he were in the know on the inside joke.

Aiden couldn't help but wonder what the blond cutie might actually know. She brushed that off and glanced at the menu. Even though Fisher somehow offered the exact appetizer she wanted, she ordered another one for the heck of it. "Could we start with the crab dip and... the crawfish ceviche?"

Kaden glanced at the basket of fritters while biting back a laugh and nodded. "Anything else?"

"You see that nice group of ladies over there?" Aiden pointed and the waiter looked over his shoulder at the table where eight older women were just being seated. "I'd like to treat them with the same appetizers, but also add the lobster stuffed prawns." It was the priciest appetizer on the menu, making her proud of the quick thinking.

He leaned over and said, "My man warned me to keep a close eye on you. This is going to be fun."

Nora, who had kept unusually mute during the entire exchange, cleared her throat after Kaden disappeared. "What are you up to now?"

"He's footing the bill, so I plan on making sure he pays and then some." She gestured around at the abundant number of customers. "He stole them from us today. That's not playing fair."

"Everything you've done to him out of spite in the last month was considered fair?" Her forehead creased, but Nora left it at that and turned her sights on the conch fritters, divvying a few out onto the small plates.

Both women paused to silently say grace before trying out the fried dough filled with minced conch and peppers and spices.

"What do you reckon is in this dipping sauce?" Aiden asked as she dunked another one into the small ramekin holding the creamy condiment before popping it into her mouth.

Nora patted the blue cloth napkin to her lips with a pondering look. "Curry and lime and coconut milk with a hint of heat, so maybe cayenne or some type of hot sauce."

Before they could even make a dent in the basket, Kaden was back with their other appetizer choices. After he delivered the appreciative older group their generous appetizers, the amused waiter was back to collect the next order choices, but they were in no hurry so he sat beside Nora and watched them sample and critique each dish. He graciously accepted bites of each appetizer, but loyally praised each one.

Aiden muttered, "Wuss," at one point, causing him to chuckle at her heckling.

"No wonder Fisher refers to you as his Little Fire all the time." He chuckled, pulling out the iPad to type in their order.

"Wonder if we should convert to iPads?" Nora asked, but Aiden barreled over the comment as though it was never spoken.

"*His* Little Fire?"

Kaden kept the overconfident smile in place. "Yep."

"I'm not his anything. You got that?" She pointed at him sternly.

"Prove it by giving me your number then," he challenged.

Who does this punk think he is? Aiden crossed her arms and cut a sharp glare over to Nora when she heard her friend snicker. *Snort, snicker, repeat.* Her hazel eyes slid back to Kaden who was just having himself such a large time at her and his idiot boss's expense. "Who trained you to treat customers so impolitely?"

"You're not a customer, but most definitely his Little Fire." The challenge was thrown down again.

"Do you people happen to have one of those old-school writing tools somewhere around here?" She heard Nora loud and clear about the iPads before interrupting, but had no desire to make that change.

Kaden produced a pen from his pocket and gladly handed it over with knowing. Aiden scribbled her number on one of the stupid coupons Nora had placed on the table and handed the challenge to him.

"I'll be calling," he promised before turning to a bemused Nora to take her order.

Nora selected the Cajun barbeque shrimp and handed over her menu, grumbling she was already getting full.

Aiden's shoulders were stubbornly set, not giving into her sated belly's protests so easily. "Nora also wants to try the lime shrimp for comparison. And I'll take the Mahi-Mahi, since I keep getting swindled out of that one." Nora snorted again, but she plowed on. "I also want the crab cakes entrée and the scallops with the avocado salsa."

Kaden reached out for the menu, but shook his head and wandered off when she refused to hand it over. He had wised up with the appetizer round and refrained from asking if they wanted anything else. Aiden bit back the smile, thinking he was probably worried she would order the scallops for another group if given the chance. She did actually think about it.

Aiden felt a little vindicated with taking full advantage of the open order, as well as having her and Nora's faces on display, effectively contradicting Fisher's claim of personal issues.

One of the café's loyal patrons walked over and placed her manicured hand on Nora's shoulder. "Sweetie, I thought one of you gals might have been under the weather or something. That sign—"

"Mrs. Powell, the sign was just a silly joke." Nora interrupted, stomping Aiden's foot and giving her a severe look, making her friend clamp her lips together and force a smile.

"Oh, good. That's such a relief. The bridge group will see you tomorrow then?" Mrs. Powell straightened the hem of her silk tunic.

"We can't wait. I've already prepared ya special dessert." Nora was so smooth, Aiden couldn't help but genuinely smile.

This line of curious inquiries continued throughout the remainder of their meal with the two women responding the same—Nora bruising Aiden's toes in warning every time she tried opening her mouth, Aiden forcing a smile, and Nora admitting the whole thing a prank.

"Remind me to never wear flip-flops out to eat with you ever again," Aiden said through gritted teeth.

"We will not add any fuel to the rumor fire. Leave well enough alone."

"How can you brush this off so easily? We keep getting the short end of the Fisher stick. That man has cut into our profit, the stupid coupon prank backfired with helping him instead of hindering…" She waved her fork up at the Fishermen's Prayer. "He got an awesome new decorative element, and he stole our recipe."

"As I said, leave well enough alone and that stick will stop getting short."

Aiden poked the key lime, coconut cake with her fork. "I don't think you made any sense on that one." She licked the cream cheese frosting off the prongs, too full to take an actual bite.

"You know what I meant." Nora took a sip of ginger ale Kaden had just delivered at her request. "What's with the two of you?"

Aiden's eyes wandered around the dining area until they landed on the other part of the two in question, watching on as he welcomed a new group of five. The annoying man looked so warm and relaxed in the white linen shirt and tan linen trousers. His hand brushed a wavy caramel lock from his forehead as he glanced in her direction. Those pouty lips pulled up smugly with catching her staring. She looked away quickly.

"Just look at him." Both women stole a quick glance, finding him chuckling over something a grey-headed man was telling him. "The man makes me want to sprawl out on top of him."

Nora choked on her ginger ale.

Aiden's cheeks went up in flames. "I meant he's so warm and inviting, like a bed…" *No, that didn't sound right either.* She cleared her throat and tried again, but Nora interrupted.

"You really are pregnant," she teased.

"Shh! Don't say that. If this town doesn't get a life soon, they're gonna successfully ruin mine." She slumped in her chair, looking around to see if anyone was eavesdropping. "Ugh. I think I'm food tipsy."

Nora snickered but it turned into a hiccup, making her sound food tipsy too.

"He's an illusion. Seems so friendly and open, but he's evil and full of trickery." *Yes, that sounded better.*

"And he confuses me." Aiden admitted on a sigh. They dropped the subject after this, much to her relief.

"This is so wasteful." Nora waved her own fork in the direction of all of the dessert dishes littering their table. "I can't believe you ordered every dessert on the menu." Her bronzed skin seemed tinged a little green as she tried to stifle a burp.

"You feel all right?" If Nora puked right there at the table, it would make Aiden's year.

"I just need some antacids." She moaned, dropping her fork. "And to never eat again."

"The food make you sick?" Aiden asked with too much enthusiastic optimism.

Nora narrowed her glassy eyes. "Knock it off." She slowly stood and began wobbling to the exit.

Aiden abandoned their table filled with half-eaten dishes and followed suit. People kept asking if Nora was okay as they passed by. Aiden would give a sympathetic look toward her friend's retreating back and whisper, "She's feeling sick. Think it may have been the ceviche."

Chapter Seven

Recipe for Jealousy
Take one exchanged number, dial it, and proceed with the
daring date. Rub it into the desired person's face until he
hits a boiling point. At that time, ease away from flame and
allow to cool.
Recipe Tip: Know when you've taken things too far, and
admit your own jealousy.

The ocean breeze seemed insistent on rushing the summer away. Festivals and other celebrations peppered the calendar for July and August. However, Fisher and Aiden seemed to be stuck back at their "impasse" and Aiden was growing weary of it.

The ceviche didn't make her sick! This was the text she received later on that night after both her and Nora had overindulged in his tasty fare. Of course, she deleted it in response.

Fisher didn't care for taking a dose of his own medicine, and kept his distance after that. Even going as far as to bringing a towel of his own to worship services and sitting as far away from her as possible. If he wanted space, then Aiden was happy granting it to him.

Well, except for that one day last month.

Anger began to bubble as she paused in mopping the café floor to rub the tender area on the back of her upper arm—another rather sore spot to add to the growing list between them. She had been minding her own business when one of her patrons, Mrs. Helen, had scooted her little old self in and gave Aiden a good tongue lashing along with the bruise on her arm. Fisher was seen wearing a sling on his left arm and the rumor spread like wildfire that Aiden had shoved him down the deck stairs over a dispute, causing him to break his collarbone.

She stormed next door and demanded him to publicly disclaim the rumor.

"You're causing a scene," he hissed, ushering her into the kitchen with his good hand while wisely keeping the injured arm out of reach.

"Well, Mrs. Helen just caused a scene in my café thanks to you!" she yelled, pulling a cringe from him.

"I didn't start the blame rumor." He gingerly adjusted the sling while keeping his scowl locked on her.

"No, but you didn't deny it when you know good and darn well I didn't break your collarbone." Her chest heaved and the flush painted vividly along her neck and cheeks. "Instead of clearing things up, you just keep telling people you rather not comment on the accident. You're intentionally making it sound like I'm guilty! I'm not guilty!"

"No need in having a conniption fit." He took a cautious step away from her rage.

Aiden yanked her sleeve up to show him the

angry red mark as she eliminated the distance he was trying to slyly put between them. "I did nothing to deserve that feisty lady pinching the fool out of me while delivering an actual lecture on keeping *my* hands to myself. Said I could have broken your stupid neck when I pushed you down the stairs!"

His lip dared to twitch in amusement and that's all it took for her to reach out and knock his arm nestled in the sling.

"*Ouch!*" he growled.

She bared her teeth before saying, "You best be glad I don't believe in voodoo or I'd be finding a way to put a hex on your Louisiana behind!" She marched out through the back, glaring a warning at the kitchen staff as they stood frozen from shock.

Come to find out, Fisher slipped on his wet boat deck and rammed his shoulder into a piece of equipment, causing the fracture. But that story didn't circulate as rampant as the fabricated version.

The sudden rain shower had vanished right before her eyes as the redhead stood staring out the front window of the café. She shook off the humiliating scene and went back to whining about his withdrawn behavior to Nora as they worked on closing up.

"It has nothing to do with that date?" The dark-haired beauty rolled her eyes.

"Why would you think that?" she sassed back, mopping around the tables. She looked up and found Nora pinning her with those perceptive green eyes.

"The text message?"

Kaden? Really? The message Fisher had sent after her dare date went ignored as well.

"Two words! He was being nosy." She turned her back and went on about mopping.

"You flaunted the date in his face in his *own* restaurant. He had no reason to be nosy." Nora shook her head and scooted back into the kitchen. "He did have grounds to be jealous," she hollered out.

The mop kept up the languid task of washing the grey and orange tiled floor while Aiden's thoughts wandered back to that date last weekend. It had been Kaden's suggestion to eat at Fishermen's Cove, maybe his little way of driving home the dare. Aiden had agreed and spent the evening listening to the young guy drone on and on about his real passion, stock-car racing. He proudly told her about a few races he'd won and how waiting tables was just temporary until he could get sponsorship.

Aiden nodded politely and managed to smile some, but awareness of a set of molten eyes watching all night kept her on edge. Each glance up, Fisher captured her in his golden snares. From the looks of him, he was none too pleased to have her back as a guest in his domain. She tried to ignore him and her uncomfortableness, by worrying a loose string at the hem of her green knee-length skirt. The date couldn't get over fast enough, in her opinion.

Kaden walked her to the door of her apartment that night, and she felt it necessary to make things clear.

Keeping her body turned to an uninviting angle,

she unlocked the door and took a step inside before saying, "I fulfilled the dare."

"How about I dare you to another one?" His smile widened to a devilish grin.

Her own smile wavered. "I had a great time, but I just don't think it's a good idea."

"You sure?" He lowered his head, trying to capture her uncooperative eyes. She nodded. "How about a goodnight kiss?"

Aiden obliged by blowing him a kiss right before closing the door in his face.

Her cheeks warmed with a new wave of embarrassment produced from the memory as she plunged the mop into the rolling bucket and began pushing it toward the back door. Brittany met her in the hallway with her purse slung over her shoulder.

"Before I head out, I wanted to let you know Fisher came by earlier."

Aiden brushed a wayward curl behind her ear and demanded herself not to respond too quickly. Everyone had razzed her about the obvious crush she had on her rival. Her cheeks warmed again when the image of the sun deity leering over her with his bronzed skin glistening in a disastrous mess flickered before her. The town held the annual Sun and Seafood Festival last weekend. Of course, Aiden and Fisher both entered dishes into the cook-off contest. Both Nora and Fisher's chef refused to take part, with having no desire to get caught up in the crossfires of their shenanigans. The committee thought it would be cute to assign the rumored couple's booths beside each other. It was fine at first with both staying stubbornly on mute.

Halfway through, Fisher broke his silence and asked how her date went with the kid.

"He's only three years younger," she snapped back before being able to stop herself.

The smug look on his face was the beginning of her undoing. While he continued to dice a tomato, she reared back and hurled a lime, making contact with his shoulder. His smugness morphed into outrage as he cut a glare at her.

"What's your problem?" They both noticed him gripping his knife in her direction, so Fisher placed it on the cutting board and tried flexing the tension from his fingers.

"You're my problem. From the day you moseyed your illusive, arrogant self into my café. You've messed with my personal and professional life," she whispered harshly with hopes of not drawing any attention.

"Me? You're the one who has done nothing but drive me absolutely crazy. Trying to sabotage my place with the rotten fish and spreading it around that Nora got sick from the ceviche." It was obvious he was still rubbed wrong.

"So stealing my recipe, being deceitful about your identity, and stealing my business was you playing nice?" She took advantage of him leaning over her station by grabbing a tomato and squishing it along the front of his T-shirt.

Fisher retaliated by swiping the mushed mess

from her grasp and returning it across the upper edge of her tank top. "You make me feel like a fool, chasing you around like a puppy dog, and then you go and throw another guy in my face!" The normal, mellow timbre of his voice roared with indignation as he dropped the mangled tomato and grabbed up a spoonful of sour cream, flicking it at her flushed face, leaving abundant speckles of white.

His actions left her no time to ponder his confession. Instead, she disregarded it and threw the first thing her hand landed on, slimy squid. The sticky creature slapped him in the forehead before sliding down his face.

With both of their tempers flaring, the situation escalated to a humiliating show right before the festival goers' entertained eyes. By the time the festival officials evicted them from the contest, both were a heaving mess of food and frustration.

"Did you hear me?" Brittany waved her hand in front of Aiden's face.

"Huh?" Aiden refocused on the waitress.

"He wanted me to give out invitations for a sunrise breakfast—"

"Brittany! I thought I made it clear last time for that not to happen again!" She dropped the mop handle and scrubbed her hands down her face.

The blonde threw her hand up to halt her boss's tantrum. "I told him no! Thank you very much."

"Oh... Well, thank you." She kicked the mop bucket, sending it colliding with the door. "I guess he hasn't stolen enough of my lunch business, so now he's going after my breakfast crowd, too!"

Brittany hitched her purse farther up her shoulder and stared at the door with longing. "I don't know..."

"When is this breakfast?"

"Next week sometime. He's hosting it on the back deck."

"The deck isn't that big." Feeling relieved, she moved over to take care of the mop water. "He can't steal too much business." As she pushed the bucket outside, a symphony of power tools revved up. She glanced over and noticed sections roped off while men worked on the additions to the deck that seemed to extend around the other side of his building. "You've got to be kidding me!" she yelled, but her voice was washed out from the whining of the skill saw and the pounding beats of hammers.

~ ☼ ~ ☼ ~ ☼ ~

The restaurant's nice new deck was complete, the town was raving over Fisher's unique menu, and the local news station came out to film a feature about his success. Everything seemed to be going right as rain for the enigmatic Phillip Moreau, causing Aiden's skin to prick with...*jealousy*?

Staring out the back window the morning of the sunrise breakfast, she shook that absurd notion off. No way was she jealous... Concerned over her profits dipping a bit from last year... Yes, definitely.

"Leave the man be and make ya coffee," Nora

ordered as she placed muffin tins filled with orange pistachio batter into the oven.

She kept her place by the window a little longer, watching the new wrought iron tables fill with guests while Fisher walked around greeting everyone. He was dressed in an aqua-blue polo shirt with the Fishermen's Cove logo and white shorts, looking like a breath of sunshine as always. Oddly enough, Fisher's usual pouty smile had been replaced with a forced one that went nowhere near his eyes. He looked over as though sensing her gaze. Their eyes held a long pause until she backed away from the window and took care of the coffee task.

"What?" Aiden pulled out the filter basket and began scooping coffee into it, realizing Nora had been rambling on the entire time.

"I'm inspired by Fisher's events," she repeated over her shoulder as her focus remained on whipping up the filling for individual quiches.

"How so?" Aiden pushed the start buttons and wiped the counter around the coffee station.

"Why don't we put together a special event here?"

Aiden scooted over to the prep table, noticing they were almost identically dressed in light-orange shirts with the café's logo dancing in cream letters on the back and boyfriend-style jean capris with their ever-present flip-flops. She swiped a piece of cheese from the ingredients before asking, "What do you have in mind?"

"How about a tasting event?"

"We're not a winery," Aiden said, stating the obvious with thick sarcasm.

"You know what I mean." Nora poured filling into the mini pie crusts and muttered, "Always gotta be so condescending."

Aiden ignored her remark and plowed on with the idea. "How about a dessert tasting?" She was really beginning to warm to the idea.

Nora snapped her fingers. "Yah. We can set up the counter as a dessert buffet."

"Desserts After Dark!" Aiden's hazel eyes widened with excitement while Nora's head nodded in exuberant agreement. Surely, this would garner the café some much needed attention.

The sun had begun to peek from the horizon, drawing Aiden back over to the window. Glancing towards the right, she watched on as Fisher stood before the group with Levi and the older gentleman she recognized from the grand opening towards his left. The older man and Fisher favored quite a bit, giving away to the fact they were probably father and son. There was also a beautiful brunette by his right side. His arm draped over her shoulder as he addressed the group. Aiden's skin began to prickle again, but when he brushed the back of his hand across his cheek, the jealousy faded and was replaced with concern. There he stood crying, and all she wanted to do was go over and offer him comfort. At that moment, the brunette gathered him in her arms and he willingly went.

"We have customers," Nora said from her

position at the stove.

Aiden gathered her wits and strode into the dining area, hoping all of her topsy-turvy emotions would straighten out sooner rather than later over that man.

Chapter Eight

Recipe of Indulgence
Take one tempting desire. Add a scoop of intrigue and mix
with a substantial portion of gumption. Blend until the
right consistency of gratification is formed.
Recipe Tip: Be careful not to over blend. Too much of any
one thing can become intolerable.

The warm glow of the lower lighting illuminated
the café in a way Aiden had never seen. It felt strange
to have a boisterous crowd mingling in the space at
night, but the gratification was overwhelming from
the event's success. It had become the talk of the
coastal town.

She pulled in a deep breath of the heavenly
aroma of citrus and chocolate as she stepped up to the
counter to add more squares of orange pound cake.

"The orange infused chocolate fountain is to die
for," Kylie, a local food blogger, boasted.

"Why thank you. Nora is a genius," Aiden
bragged, giving the credit where it rightfully
belonged. Her eyes swept over the fountain serving
as the centerpiece with various treats displayed at the
base for dipping.

Nora was rearranging a platter of lemon glazed

petit fours, but glanced up to accept the praise with a grateful smile.

The food blogger dunked another homemade marshmallow through the decadent cascade of chocolate. "Please say this isn't just a one-time event."

The two café owners exchanged a look. Nora shrugged. "I don't see why we can't pull this off at least three or four times a year. Maybe with a seasonal theme?"

Aiden nodded. "I like that idea. That's frequent enough to satiate people, but not so much the event becomes mundane."

Kylie made note in her notepad and continued sampling the bounty of desserts. The large gathering gravitated around the counter, filling their plates, and then mingled around the dining area or out on the back deck. The set of glass doors at the back of the dining area were rarely left opened, but the night called for it so that the sea breeze was allowed to waft around the special occasion.

"My mouth won't stop watering," Brittany groaned as she gave in and snuck a chunky orange and white chocolate blondie. She let out a satisfying moan, causing her two boss ladies to giggle.

The young blonde had grown on them throughout the summer, and she seemed quite attached to them as well, spending most of her free time hanging out with them. Brittany even volunteered to help out that night.

Aiden gave into temptation and dipped an orange segment through the molten chocolate while admiring the jovial gathering. All of the paid ads, the street team efforts with handing out flyers, and some sneaky placements of advertising had greatly paid off. It made her admit that change had to happen in order to see growth. She wondered if the feeling of trepidation mixed with anticipation was how Aunt Donna also felt when she handed over the keys to her. Smiling at the thought, she pulled her phone out of the pocket of her dressy capris and snapped several pictures before sending them to her aunt.

Every guest left later on with dainty bags of sweets donated by the sweet shop across the street and satisfied bellies. The night was nothing shy of successful, but boy had it been exhausting. Aiden glanced at the clock displaying the time just shy of eleven, and calculated that she had clocked in a grand total of eighteen hours.

"Thank heavens tomorrow is Sunday," she muttered to herself as she placed a few more plates into the bin.

She had literally pushed Nora and the wait staff out of the door earlier. They gladly dragged their tired selves out with promising to stop by late tomorrow afternoon to do the prep work for Monday.

As she moved to the next table, Aiden realized she forgot to lock up the front. She shuffled over, but before she could turn the lock, the door swung open to produce an annoyed Phillip Moreau.

"Ugh. I'm in no mood to deal with you tonight," Aiden said through gritted teeth as she tried futilely to push him back out of the door.

"Tough." Fisher eased around her and began rolling up the sleeves of his blue button-down he had paired with khaki shorts and tanned Sperry top siders. Spotting the nearly cleaned-out dessert display, he made a beeline to it. "Did you leave me any?"

When he appeared to not be leaving anytime soon, Aiden reluctantly closed the door. "Why would I do that?"

He ignored her snarky reply and shoved several caramel dipped apple wedges into his mouth. "You have a thing for caramels," he garbled out, calling her on the obvious. "Man, there's hardly anything left.

"We pretty much sold out." She limped over to him, glad he didn't linger on the caramel subject. Her comparing him to decadent caramel had clearly made its way to him. People liked to talk too much in the small town, in her opinion.

"Totally understandable beings I didn't sell one blame dessert all night." His words grouched out as he popped several petit fours in his mouth, effectively cleaning the platter. "I'm still baffled by how you managed to tape those cards about this thing over my desserts in each menu." He cut her a suspicious look. "Clever."

Aiden was a little ashamed about pulling that off with the aid of the teenage boy busing tables. The young guy had heard about the epic pranks both of them had been pulling off and naively agreed to be part of one.

She shook her head, watching on as he kept

sampling. The man looked way too comfortable in her space. He paused at the fountain, grabbing a skewer and stabbing several cake squares and marshmallows with it a bit too forcefully for Aiden's likings. He managed to gather some leftover chocolate from the bottom of the fountain along the loaded skewer and went to work on devouring it.

Aiden pulled in a long breath, holding it tightly before slowly freeing it as she eased around the counter to unplug the fountain. Her hope was that he would see that as his sign to go away and leave her alone.

"Why are you limping?" he asked around a mouthful of cake, watching her hobble back to his side.

"I've been on my feet since six this morning."

"That's why you should stick to your regular hours. It's too much."

His dominant tone didn't do anything but tick her off even more. Her hands settled sternly on her hips as she glared up at him. "I'm a grown woman. It's none of your business what I do." She glanced over at the counter. "And just who do you think you are, coming in here and helping yourself like this?" She waved a hand toward the empty dishes left in his grazing wake.

Fisher smirked his chocolate covered lips at her. "I was helping you clean up." Licking his lips, he released a deep moan as he moved closer. "I love how husky your voice becomes when you get all riled up."

Aiden's mouth began to water as he settled his

hand over her hand still perched on her hip. Her quick intake of breath caused his lips to widen and his eyes to narrow as he gave her a smug look.

"I don't know if I want to smack that smirk of your lips or kiss it off."

Both went still from her confession.

"Did I just say that out loud?" Mortified, she tried to take a step back, but he kept her firmly in place. She was so tired of the man driving her to distraction.

"Oh yeah. And I'd much rather we go for the latter." Licking his lips once more, he leaned forward.

With the aroma of decadent chocolate on his breath and the ever-present warmth of his touch, Aiden's mind tripped all over with indecision and nervousness. Panicked, she reached over, grabbed a brownie, and shoved it into his too-close mouth.

Chewing, he released her and propped his side against the counter, seemingly satisfied with the effect he had on her. "I'm looking forward to when you finally find the gumption to follow through on that kissing threat. I guarantee it'll be more delicious than that brownie."

"Why are you really here?" She yawned as she watched him grab a napkin and wipe away the chocolate smudges around his mouth from the brownie.

He flicked the napkin on the counter. "We need to knock this mess off already."

Well, that woke her up. "We? No, *you*! You're the one who started this. And you're the one that just keeps right on at it. That sunrise breakfast robbed almost all of my breakfast sales that morning."

Now it was Fisher's turn to look frustrated. Crossing his arms he pinned her with an irritated stare. "Stealing your business had nothing to do with that breakfast. It'll also be only an annual event, so don't go get all whiny about it."

Her business sense kicked in. "Why only once a year? It was a hit."

"Contrary to what you believe, I'm not out to sabotage your café and everything I do ain't about you, sweetheart."

She opened her mouth to rebuttal, but he held his hand up.

"It was to honor my late mother's birthday. You'd have known that if you had accepted my invitation."

"We thought you were trying to get us to pass them out..."

"No, I offered her only one invite, but she said no."

Feeling right ridiculous, Aiden hung her head, but peeped up to apologize. "Oh... I'm so sorry. Honestly, I didn't know. Brittany was only doing what I told her to do."

Fisher's expression filled with somberness as he nodded. "Mom's only been gone two years. We all still miss her like it was just yesterday. One of my favorite memories is her meeting us at the docks with a hearty breakfast in tow." His words trailed off as a shaky smile ghosted his lips. He absently ran his fingers along the surface of the smooth counter while his memories took him miles away and up the coast.

"She always made us the best salmon and potato hash. I gave the recipe to my chef for the sunrise breakfast. Dude nailed it. I took one bite that morning and had to excuse myself to get my emotions back into check. My dad said a few words and we celebrated her by doing what she would have found joy in, us pigging out on good food. Mom would have approved." He met her gaze with watery eyes.

Aiden stepped over their invisible line and wrapped him in a hug when the desire to comfort him overtook her. The hug began in a tense awkwardness before settling into a soothing caress. It only took seconds for Fisher to get over the shock of her actions, his stiff back relaxed as he returned her embrace.

He tucked his face into his favorite spot, the crook of her neck, and inhaled slowly. "No woman has ever fit me like you do, Little Fire." His words were muffled as he snuggled closer to her. "I know you're off limits, but my arms sure want to beg to differ."

She didn't know how to respond to that. Instead, she said what had been on her mind for weeks. "I was worried about you, especially after you didn't respond to my message." She indulged further by running her fingers through his silky locks, provoking a deep moan to vibrate through his chest.

He remained burrowed to the side of her neck as he said, "I know." The warm breath his words brought forth caused a tingle to skirt along her skin. "Figured I'd give you a taste of how it felt to be ignored."

His arrogant sass snapped her out of the tender moment. Aiden tried pushing him off, but Fisher refused to budge. "Err! I should have known better." She kept squirming and pushing and he kept her clamped securely in his arms. "You don't need any comfort from me anyway. Seems you had a pretty brunette offering you plenty that morning."

Fisher yanked his head up and grinned. Those caramel eyes gleamed in satisfaction. "Are you jealous?"

"No!" She shoved him fruitlessly.

"I don't believe you."

"Well, I don't like you!" She growled while struggling to free herself.

"Such a fibber." He tsked as his hand reached up and freed her red curls from the hairclip. His fingers began kneading along her tender scalp, stilling her protest almost instantly.

Aiden's eyes lost focus and the long day seemed to catch up with her all of a sudden. "Fisher..."

"That beautiful brunette is my sister Madilyn."

"Oh."

He swallowed deeply before continuing. "Aiden, no woman has captured my attention since that first day you stole it."

She wanted to argue who stole what that day, but she was too close to drooling to protest. Her head lobbed forward until her forehead rested against his chest before making a confession of her own. "The date was a dare. I agreed to it to get back at you."

Aiden waited for him to laugh and tease her, but

his unexpected reaction caught her off guard. Before she could protest, Fisher had her thrown over his shoulder, marching outside to the deck.

"Now what are you doing?" She growled her words while slapping him on the back as the humid breeze pushed her hair into her face.

Placing her onto a lounge chair, Fisher sat on the end and began ridding the confused woman of her shoes as she pushed her wild hair out of her eyes. She set a glare on her face, but he was too busy with the task at hand to pay the attitude any mind.

"Flip-flops are a sorry choice for long hours of standing."

The retort was on the tip of her tongue, but got stuck there when his strong hands captured a sore foot and began massaging. The snappy words were replaced with a long, luxuriating moan. His soothing touch on her sore feet as he kneaded her heel was so heavenly, Aiden's brain took a timeout and forgot all about hating him.

"Why—"

"Shh," he interrupted, moving to her left foot.

With the lullaby of the ocean waves dancing on the shore and the warmth of his touch, Aiden floated into a languid slumber...

"Hey."

A hand caressed the sleepy woman's cheek. Before her eyes managed to open, she dozed back off.

"Aiden."

"Hmm?" Slowly opening her eyes, she took in Fisher stretched out beside her in the lounge chair, the soft glow of the nightlight sweeping across his handsome face.

"I hated to wake you, but it's three in the morning. We should probably head home."

She sat up to get her bearings and discovered a linen tablecloth serving as a blanket tucked around her body. "We've been out here that long?" she asked in disbelief.

"You have." Fisher stood and helped Aiden to her feet.

It didn't register what he had said until they entered the café. She came to a halt, finding the entire counter spotless as well as the tables with the chairs resting on top. Her eyes moved to the floor and noticed the tiles were still slightly damp.

"Fisher, why'd you do all this? You didn't have to."

"Because I really want to be your friend. Do you think that's a possibility?"

She looked over and found hope lighting his features. "We could try." She shrugged.

He released a soft chuckle. "Okay. Let me drive you home."

Every stubborn protest yammered in her ear, but Aiden ignored it and shocked them both when she accepted.

Fisher drove her home in silence. Parking in front of the apartment, he asked, "Would you like me to walk you to the door?"

She realized he was respecting her strong-mindedness by allowing her the choice. Maybe they had come to understand each other in those last four rocky months more than she realized. Aiden looked over and noticed his eyes trained on her mouth. Clearly, he wanted more than friendship, but Aiden wasn't ready to breach those waters.

"Thanks, but I'm good."

"Okay." His shoulders slumped slightly.

Aiden wanted to offer some assurance, so she reached over and squeezed his hand before hopping out of the truck. Once she was inside, she waited to hear his truck pull away. Several minutes passed before that occurred, making her wonder what he was out there thinking about so hard. She knew there was a lot she needed to think about.

Chapter Nine

Time-tested Recipe for Trust
Begin with a confident helping of faith. Add in some consideration for flaws, while eliminating the portion of doubt from the recipe altogether. Double the amount of actual honesty and slowly combine, allowing time to proof the process.
Recipe Tip: Keep in mind that mistakes happen, so that past imperfections are not allowed to ruin the hopeful future.

Waking up in order to make Sunday's worship service was no easy feat. Her achy feet and tired brain begged her to remain in the comforts of the warm bed, but Aiden reminded herself that the entire afternoon could be spent resting afterwards. After sleepwalking through a long, hot shower to work the kinks out of her neck and shoulders, Aiden decided to forgo blow drying her hair and gave permission to the wild beast to do as she pleased for the day. She tossed on a pair of white Bermuda shorts and a teal peasant blouse, calling it done.

Too tired to peddle her worn-out behind to the café, she loaded up in her tiny Prius for the less-than-five-minute drive. As she parked at the curb, Aiden took a moment to regard both the café and Fishermen's Cove—both in grey tones with splashes of well-placed color. The buildings also had similar tin roofs and large black planters brimming over with tropical plants. She couldn't hold back the smile, realizing he had finally put the planters back out front.

"Humph..." She leaned her head back as an unnerving feeling tightened her chest. "The two buildings actually complement each other, like a perfectly coordinated pair," she muttered to herself.

Shaking off the peculiar notion that God was trying to tell her something, Aiden climbed out of the car and scooted through the alley with hopes of sneaking on her back deck undetected. She spotted Fisher reclined in a chair with his feet propped up on her deck railing, his ankles crossed casually with his hands resting behind his head. Instead of climbing the steps, she paused to watch him. The weird tightening in her chest grew when she realized his outfit coordinated with her own except his shirt was white and his long shorts were teal.

"Stop thinking about running off and get your cute self up here," he said in a languid tone that seemed to still be holding on to sleep.

Exhaling, Aiden timidly made the short trek up and across the deck before slouching in the awaiting chair beside him. Fisher eased a leg down, hooked his ankle under her chair, and dragged her closer. Several service attendees paused to wave at the pair on the deck before settling down on their beach towels. They threw a hand up, returning the friendly gesture.

"I can hear the gossip already for tomorrow," Aiden whispered for fear the groups' listening ears would hear.

Fisher dropped his arms and offered Aiden his hand. "Who cares?"

Aiden gave his hand a sidelong glance, but didn't accept it.

"Hold my hand," his husky voice demanded.

"Why?"

"Honestly, I'm drawn to your touch. You have a warmth that lingers, even when you're being feisty."

"Says the man created from sunshine." She glanced up and was caught in the snare of those gold pools. The man's expression held so much sincerity she could hardly stand it. After contemplating the offer longer than it necessitated, she placed her hand into his. Instinctively, his long fingers wrapped around hers. The warmth of his gentle touch traveled through her entire body. Blinking at the curious sensation, Aiden could have sworn his delicate sunshine had just kissed her soul.

"You feel it, too," he whispered.

With her eyes remaining locked on their joined hands, she asked, "What?"

"This." Fisher lightly squeezed her hand. "And finally allowing the possibility…"

Before he finished his declaration or Aiden could ask what he meant or confess that she wasn't comfortable exploring any types of possibilities, the music ceased and the preacher began to share God's message. She settled in and tried her best to listen. She could barely refrain the snort when he stated the message would reflect on listening to what God is trying to tell us through His words and through signs.

"Are you listening?" Preacher Jeff asked with exuberance. Murmurings swept through the group as he flipped through the pages of his weathered Bible. He stopped on a page and began reading, "I will listen to what God the Lord will say; he promises peace to his people, his saints, but let them not return to folly." He held his Bible high in the air, the ocean breeze dancing with the thin pages. "We've all made mistakes. Not one of us can truthfully oppose my claim. But He gives us the instructions on how to live in peace. It's up to us to listen to His words and not make the same mistakes again."

Aiden absently rubbed her thumb along Fisher's palm as she took in the message. She contemplated the mess with her ex-fiancé Neal, vowing to never make that mistake again. Holding Fisher's hand should have reminded her, a warning, but never had holding someone's hand felt so natural. Never had any experience come close to the emotions bubbling through her that sunny Sunday morning.

The preacher concluded with something along the lines of trusting your instincts and always aligning your actions with God's instructions. Fisher let out an *amen* while giving Aiden a pointed look. She shocked both of them when her head nodded in agreement instead of the normal glare.

As a closing prayer was offered, Fisher abruptly

stood, pulling her along with him, and hustled over to his place and through the back door.

"What are you doing?" Aiden asked as soon as he flipped the lock.

"Dodging the crowd before they're let loose." He dropped her hand and began gathering ingredients.

Aiden followed behind him. "Now what are you doing?"

Fisher turned from the fridge and took her in as though it were the first time he had seen her all day, making her feel admired, yet at the same time, uncomfortable. "Aiden, would you please spend the afternoon with me and let me cook you a meal?"

The softened timbre of his voice and the optimistic look he was giving her made it impossible to decline the offer. She glanced around the space. Although fatigue from yesterday still worried her, she nodded in agreement.

In a hammock several miles down the coast, Aiden's belly was comfortably full with fish tacos made fresh by Fisher and coconut cake he swiped from the restaurant.

"I can't believe I've agreed to this," she slurred out in her almost comatose state, her head resting on her host's shoulder.

"You have to admit coming over to my house was a good idea." His fingers roamed a lazy path through her curly hair.

"I guess… It was nice not having any snooping eyes watching us." She peeked open her heavy lids and admired the view of the tranquil sandy beach, shaded by massive palm trees. She was surprised when he drove his truck through a gated beach community earlier. He had shrugged it off, saying he needed privacy after being in the public eye all day, even if it meant paying through the nose for it. It was a new lifestyle for him, having spent most of his life on a secluded boat. She toyed with the fringe on the hammock, thinking she could totally relate. "You know I get asked at least twice a day where my engagement ring is." Her elbow playfully teased his side.

Fisher's deep chuckle warmed her. "Yeah. I get asked when is the wedding a good bit. I figured after our public display of hate at that festival, that rumor would have been put to rest."

She stretched her relaxed limbs before snuggling closer, eyes drooping shut again. "Nope. Lovers' quarrel is what the ladies over at the salon declared it and the town went right along with it."

Fisher toyed with her fingers as they rested on his chest. "Speaking of engagements… I'd like to hear your version of this runaway bride tale."

"Ugh." She tried rolling away, but he locked his arm in order to keep her. "This town needs to learn how to hush their mouths. You're lucky you're not from around here. Not much about you has circulated around yet."

"Except for our upcoming nuptials." His lips

curved in a wry smile.

"Well, I'm sure you're relieved to know I'll leave you at the altar." Her eyes rolled to add to the sarcastic effect.

"I just don't see you being that fickle about a commitment. Something else went down besides you getting cold feet." His eyes drifted shut, giving her the only type of space he was willing to offer.

"Neal stole my heart, promised me the world, as well as his commitment to love me. He failed." Her words flew out rapidly as though it were a practiced speech she was dying to get out of the way.

"If the town's recollection is correct, that's been six years ago and you're still protecting the jerk." He kept his eyes closed, seemingly to help her open up.

Aiden's own eyes remained open and roamed his striking features—dark scruff defining his jawline, pouty lips pressed firmly shut, thick lashes grazing his high cheekbones. Her perusing came to a halt when she noticed the line furrowing his forehead. That little indicator gave away his true feelings on the subject. Her shoulders shrugged defensively. "I'm not protecting him. I'm trying to protect my heart from being deceived ever again."

His eyes drew slightly open to gaze down at her. Releasing her hand, his fingers swept an errant curl away from her somber face. "Wish he still lived around here so I could punch him." The town had filled him in on quite a lot, and it was obvious he knew how to read between lines. "Guess that explains your trust issue."

With Aiden's defenses already up, she bolted off the hammock, sending Fisher flailing to the ground from being caught off guard. His body smacked the sand in a muted thud, knocking the wind out of him.

She glared down at him with her chin jutted defiantly out. "Trust is something earned. You've done nothing to earn mine since we've met!"

The fuming redhead attempted to stomp off, but before any progress was made, Fisher jumped to his feet and grasped her arm.

"I think it's time we fix this."

"How do *you* plan on going about that?"

Scratching his brow, he looked around as though the ocean or sand may hold the answer. "*We* need to earn each other's trust. Only way to do that is with time proving we're worthy of it."

"Four months have already come and gone with no proof." She cast her attention to a hermit crab scouring the shore.

Fisher tilted his head in an attempt to meet her distracted eyes. "Still such a fibber." That got those eyes snapping up to meet his, so he plowed on. "Sure, the last four months we didn't get off on the right foot. Let some silly rivalry and dumb pranks distract us from us, but look where we already are, Little Fire." He pulled her in for a hug, emphasizing his point. "You trusting me to hold you is proof."

"I'm not ready to give any more than that..." Her voice trailed off on a jagged sigh.

"Time. That's all I ask of you." His lips pressed against her hair. "Can I have it?"

As they stood anchored together underneath the protectiveness of the palm trees, Aiden weighed his request. It wasn't a demand of handing over her blemished heart, just a request to see if trust could lead back to it.

Eventually, she lifted her head to try to conjure an answer. Stalling, she bit down on her bottom lip, but his gentle fingers reached out and freed it with wanting an answer. Those gold eyes held a vulnerability that begged for a response, so she gave him one in true Aiden fashion.

"I reckon so, or you'll just steal it anyway," she sassed, causing him to laugh in relief.

"You know me too well." As he continued to hold her gaze, Fisher coasted the tips of his fingers along her cheek until they reached the corner of her mouth. "Will it ruin the progress of your trust in me too much, if I stole just one more thing I've really been wanting since the day I met you?"

Before Aiden could protest, those pouty lips crashed down on her surprised ones with such heat and passion, she melted right into it. Instantly, the sensation of sunshine radiated throughout her body and all the way to her heart, illuminating all of the darkness life-letdowns had etched there.

He said he was stealing just one more thing, but in that very moment Aiden couldn't lie to herself any longer. Phillip Moreau had successfully stolen her heart.

Chapter Ten

Best Recipe for Surrender
Take a heaping amount of thoughtful consideration while discarding any remnants of a grudge. Next, add a well-rounded scoop of appreciation for the good and a dollop of acceptance for the established differences. Fold in a smidgen of humbleness to make recipe sweeter and most appealing.
Recipe Tip: You will yield the best results if you commit to it wholeheartedly.

"I'm going to beat that man within an inch of his life!" Aiden yelled as she stormed through the back entrance of the café.

Nora kept mixing custard for the French toast casserole that was on special. "No need to yell. Nothing wrong with my hearing."

"But he's told everyone we're getting married next weekend! On Mardi Gras no less!"

"If a nuh so, a nearly so." Nora offered an unperturbed shrug.

"How can you say that? It's not close enough to being true and you know it! Stop using your grandma's sayings!"

"He's not even in town. How's he supposed to be telling all of this?"

Aiden raked her hands through her hair aggressively. "Little lady Helen stopped me on the beach just now, wanting to know why she didn't receive her invitation. Said she heard Fisher telling the cashier at the sweet shop last week. Poor woman was upset, too."

Nora snickered. "He's just messing with people, getting back at them for stirring up all those rumors about the two of you."

"Yes, but he goes running off on a fishing trip as soon as he starts it. I could kill him." She paced a path until stopping to snag a cup of coffee.

"Shouldn't the guys be back anytime now?" Nora's eyes searched for the time on the clock.

"Yes." Aiden leaned on the counter and took another sip from her steaming cup.

"Then why don't you get down to the docks and give him a piece of your mind."

"Or you could just go down there and give him a proper welcome home like the good wife you are," Brittany added as she pushed through the kitchen door from the dining area.

"Ha-ha," Aiden said, rolling her eyes. The rumor had also circulated that the two secretly married last fall, which was also not true.

"Stop giving that man a hard time already," Brittany said sternly, arms crossed. She had taken over the role of mother hen in their group.

"Fine! I'm going." She pushed off the counter and headed out.

"Go get him, girl!" Nora cheered with Brittany

hooting behind her in agreement.

Aiden ignored them and headed next door. She pulled her key out and let herself in to grab one of his blue linen napkins. They had exchanged keys a while back with Aiden letting in the early morning orders at Fishermen's, and Fisher dropping off fresh seafood and other treats for Aiden after café hours. She glanced at the Fisherman's Prayer hanging in his quiet dining area, thinking of how far they had come since then, offering it a genuine smile before leaving.

The seagulls squawked overhead as Aiden settled on a bench near the end of the dock. A nervous flicker danced in her belly as she watched the beastly 72 feet long boat glide into the marina. She spotted Fisher right away with his hat turned backwards, his focus on preparing the boat to dock right along with his crew. This was his element, and it never ceased to fascinate Aiden with seeing him this way.

Time is what he asked for and time was what she gave him. Her thoughts slanted back to how time had proven itself, in several ways. It proved that the pranks wouldn't go away, but they were directed privately, and in no way pertained to the two restaurants any longer.

Aiden tentatively picked her hand up and sniffed it, thanking the Good Lord that repulsive stench hadn't returned. She didn't realize until too late that Fisher had doused her favorite hand lotion she kept on her desk with rancid fish oil. It took forever to rid her hands of the hideous odor. She had gotten him back the following Sunday. Before she left his house, the sneaky woman set several alarm clocks she purchased at a dime store to go off every half hour after midnight. She took it a step further by hiding the alarms in various spots all around his room—dresser drawers, TV cabinet, behind the headboard, in various shoes scattered along his floor...

Her laughter faded while watching the sunrays tickle the tops of the ocean waves, but a smile remained with thinking of all the sweet moments she had acquired along the way.

Time had also proven she could trust him with her flawed heart. Caramels were a frequent delivery. The note that accompanied them always said the same thing. *Never stop thinking of me.* And she always sent a text immediately that was also always the same. *Always thinking of you.*

Time had also been sneaky with several months passing as the two got to know each other. They spent most every Sunday sharing a beach towel at service and then sharing a private meal at his home. She came to view that secluded time away from public eyes as a generous gift in itself, both letting their guards down enough to be able to relax into the friendship.

Taking a deep breath to muster up some bravery, Aiden knew her time was up. It was time to let him know how things were going to be. She kept her eyes trained on Fisher until he finally looked up and noticed her. His face lit up full of sunshine, instantly warming her. He catapulted over the side of the boat and landed gracefully onto the deck. Without missing a beat, he eliminated the distance between them in only a few long strides.

She lifted the napkin and waved it in surrender, causing him to halt. He knew what that meant and the grin pulled so broad on those pouty lips it made his eyes squint.

"Shouldn't you be waving a white flag?"

She shrugged her shoulder. "I thought using your napkin would be more symbolic."

"It's about time," he said with more authority than the moment warranted, as he took a step closer, brushing his legs against hers.

She let it slide and voiced her own opinion. "This is going to be a lot of hard work going into this partnership together. You realize we'll probably end up killing each other."

"I'm up for the challenge." He offered his arm to help her stand. As she grasped around the crook of his arm, he pulled her close, securing her firmly to his side with no apparent intentions of ever letting go.

Aiden didn't mind one bit.

She reached up and caressed his lips with her own, surrendering to trust the love God had placed in her heart for this incredibly annoying man.

As they began walking down the dock, Aiden pushed into his side. "You need to explain to Mrs. Helen that the Mardi Gras wedding was a joke."

"Who said I was kidding?" He looked down with mischief twinkling in his caramel eyes.

"I just agreed to marry you not even five minutes ago, but I did *not* agree to do it next week."

"We'll see about that," he said as they reached his truck. After opening the door, he went straight to rummaging around in the glove box until unearthing the ring box. "You *gonna* wear it now, Little Fire. No arguing this time."

He had offered it before Christmas and she had refused it. Defeated but determined, Fisher offered her more time. Almost two months more time to be exact and she knew he wouldn't be persuaded to grant her request to not wear the ring just yet. The first sight of that ring on her finger from a local would surely blow up the gossip lines.

He read her mind in that moment as he had become an expert at doing as of late. Slipping the ring on her finger, he pulled out his phone. "Let's be the first to start the gossip this time." He pulled Aiden close as she held up her hand. Before snapping the selfie, he crashed his lips against hers. He clicked several before they parted and checked to see what he captured. With toothy grins they looked at each proudly. "Let's post it on our social media pages," he mumbled while doing just that. He had hacked her sites so many times that he knew all of the passwords from memory.

Aiden knew one thing with certainty. Having Phillip Moreau in her life was undoubtedly a recipe for one interesting adventure.

~☼**Part 2**☼~

Chapter Eleven

Recipe for a Perfect Bride
Begin by finding the perfect dress and then add the perfectly romantic hairstyle. Compliment these two ingredients with a soft pallet of makeup. Round out the perfection with a tasteful amount of fine jewelry and one pair of spectacular shoes.
Recipe Tip: Remember, less is more.

"I hate this dress!" Aiden declared, tugging the bodice up once again. "This darn thing will be the death of me by the end of this day." She released the satiny neckline and it instantly rebelled by sliding back down to expose more cleavage than the redhead was comfortable with sharing.

"Quit ya fussing, ya eaz-haad!" Nora's cappuccino skin warmed several shades with frustration. "You look fine!"

"Me stubborn?" Aiden jabbed a finger in her friend's direction. "You're a fine one to talk, you little Jamaican Jerk." Her wild auburn curls vibrated, looking barely contained in the soft updo. She admired her dear friend and business partner's straightforwardness most of the time, but not on this particular day.

Nora smoothed her sleek chignon, looking totally opposite of her frazzled friend, and turned to the mirror to inspect her own gown. "You're the one who picked the dress out in the first place."

"I just don't recall it being so slippery." Aiden tugged the top once more, attaining the same results as the last several dozen attempts.

"And you're the one who had to go on a senseless diet before the wedding." Nora turned back and studied her squirming friend. "Looks like all five pounds were lost in the boobs."

Aiden threw her hands up and let out a low growl. "I give up. Let's go get this over with already." Without waiting for a reply, she stomped out of the back room of the church they were using as a makeshift dressing room.

"This should be fun," Nora mumbled, shaking her head as she grabbed up both her and Aiden's bouquet and followed behind her firecracker of a friend.

With the soft melody from the piano and a not-so-soft nudge from the wedding director, Aiden began her nervous waltz down the aisle, following behind the two bridesmaids in pale mint-green gowns, one of which was her young friend Brittany. Aiden shuffled behind the blonde beauty, begging her frantic nerves to take a break. The perfumed aroma of floral arrangements met with her, but she ignored its pleasantries, too wrapped up in the discomfort of the moment. A fine sheen of sweat brushed her skin all at once. The new dewy layer seemed to be working in her favor by causing the silky material of the gown to cling to her body. A cursory glance showed no evident sweat stains, so she allowed her eyes a tentative glance around the sanctuary. Smiling faces were trained on her, but she wasn't able to return the smile. Her own face was frozen in a blank façade, holding her trepidation inside like a prisoner.

"Walk," the director whispered harshly, making Aiden aware that she had stopped making progress down the aisle.

"Uh-oh. Here she goes *again*," one of the town's little gossiping hens clucked from a back pew.

The woman's snide remark was sufficient in ticking Aiden off enough to send her moving forward *again*. Her eyes picked back up on perusing the sanctuary until becoming caught in the snares of liquid caramel, triggering a summersault to happen in her belly. Those hypnotic eyes released her long enough to coast the length of her body, noticeably stuttering at the dangerously slipping top, before recapturing her cautious gaze.

For a man made straight from sunshine and surf, Phillip Moreau had somehow managed to look as frigid and looming as an iceberg. Neither of which Aiden had any desire to tangle with, but that day left no choice. Her only option was to move forward where he stood at the end of the seemingly long aisle. In his pristine tux and radiating a sullen demeanor, Phillip looked nowhere close to the laidback Fisher she had come to know and love. With a curt nod of his head, he released Aiden from his magnetic stare and drew his focus behind her.

Aiden blinked back the stinging in her eyes and picked up her pace to finish out the aisle marathon like a champ. She glanced at Fisher's best buddy Levi, who stood beside him. Both men looked debonair in their black tuxedos. Levi gave her a sympathetic smile before moving his gaze away from her as well.

"Let us all stand," the preacher requested.

A soft murmur swept the congregation as all turned to watch the elegant bride begin her more gracious waltz with the aisle than her maid of honor. As Nora made her way to her awaiting groom, the Jamaican beauty's face beamed with happiness and hope.

Aiden couldn't help but smile, thinking that was exactly the look a bride should have on her wedding day. She made the mistake of allowing a quick look at Fisher and found him watching her with an icy glare, eliciting a shiver to skirt along her clammy skin and causing the smile to stumble before completely falling from her face.

Nora handed over her bouquet to Aiden before sliding her hands into Levi's. The couple watched each other with heartfelt grins as the preacher began to officiate the ceremony.

Today was Nora's day, but Aiden found her skin tingling from the scrutiny of the congregation. Those curious eyes kept ping-ponging back and forth between Aiden and her estranged fiancé.

I will not cause a scene... I will not cause a scene... The silent chant continued in repetition as a bead of sweat wiggled loose and dripped down her back.

"We are gathered here today in the sight of God, and in the presence of friends and loved ones, to celebrate one of life's ultimate moments. We are here to give recognition to the worth and beauty of love, and to celebrate the commitment Levi and Nora have made to each other. Today we will witness them unite in holy matrimony," Preacher Jeff began, but was interrupted by a sullen scoff from Fisher.

A scalding heat skirted across Aiden's cheeks, climbing all the way to the tips of the redhead's earlobes as she delivered a blazing warning in her scowl. Fisher, in return, delivered sheer ice with his own glare.

"Ease up on ya self," Nora whispered over her shoulder, warning Aiden to chill out.

I will not cause a scene... I will not cause a scene...

Aiden locked her focus on the bouquet of creamy white roses and orange blossoms resting in her sweaty grip and kept it there until the groom kissed his bride. Thankfully, it was a rather short ceremony. Simple, yet elegant, mirroring the bride's taste.

As the newly married couple led the bridal procession down the aisle toward the exit, cheers of joy broke out through the crowd. Levi, over the moon with pride and excitement, grabbed Nora up into his arms and carried her out.

As soon as Aiden eased to the best man's side and claimed his arm, the bitter tension eased away. Fisher's crisp cologne reminded her of the savory ocean, hypnotizing the maid of honor into forgetting their recent riff. There was no stopping her body from gravitating closer to her personal sun. She wanted nothing more than to pretend what happened never occurred so that they could go back to openly loving each other. Not even his surly huff discouraged her from snuggling closer to his side. Their shared waltz back down the aisle and the affection she lavished out had the guests scrutinizing the estranged couple and whispering. No doubt the gossip lines would be burning up, but Aiden was greedy enough for his touch to deal with that later.

Once the doors of the church shut behind them, Fisher untangled himself from Aiden's side and stalked off while muttering, "I can't keep up with this anymore."

"Ladies and gentlemen, help me welcome Mr. and Mrs. Levi Mitchel!" The DJ's jovial voice boomed through the sound system as the couple rushed through the entrance of the Orange Blossom Café. He then cranked up the music to add to the celebration.

The newlyweds wore huge grins as they commenced with taking their first dance right away in the center of the cleared dining area. The lace of Nora's gown floated around as Levi twirled her, causing the normally reserved woman to giggle like a little girl.

Aiden watched by the counter and couldn't contain her own giggle, so happy her dearest friend had found her happiness. She nearly choked on it when she caught the severe stare of Fisher. Arms crossed and bowtie undone, he stood near the front entrance looking like he wanted to bolt.

"Alright, let's have the best man and maid of honor join the dance," the DJ announced, causing Fisher's scowl to transform into pure angst.

Aiden ignored it and met him halfway, all the while keeping up her silent chant.

I will not cause a scene… I will not cause a scene…

As soon as her hand interlaced with her handsome foe's outreached one, murmurings rippled throughout the café. No doubt, the guests would have plenty to *share* next week. Two turns in and Aiden could sense him building up to words, evident in a few halted breaths as though he was almost there but kept backing out. She patiently waited, begging herself to behave, while taking in the ivory material draped over the tables and the creamy floral centerpieces resting on top. Those delicate touches mingled beautifully with the rustic furniture and grey teak walls of the café. Nora kept the décor simple and charming for the reception, much to Aiden's approval.

Finally, Fisher said, "I see you're still wearing the ring." His comment had them both inspecting the diamond ring. It sparkled from her hand where it rested on his shoulder.

"Why wouldn't I?" The words came out huskier than her normal as nervousness tightened around her throat.

"You left me at the altar," he squeezed the words out in a painful whisper.

"I agreed to marry you, but I'm not putting up with you pushing a wedding on me." Her husky voice came out in a hiss this time. "How dare you guilt-trip me."

Fisher had tried forcing her "I do" hand by setting up a surprise wedding on the beach. She sure showed him she wouldn't be pushed into anything by storming away. Unfortunately, she showed a majority of the citizens of the small Floridian beach town, too.

Fisher's back stiffened as his glare left her. Aiden looked around to see what had drawn his attention away, finding the crowd easing closer to where they were barely dancing.

Before Aiden could snap at the nosey crowd to mind their business, the DJ announced for everyone to join in. Of course, the estranged couple had quite a few pairs dancing in close proximity.

Aiden's jaw unlocked to warn them to back off, when she heard Fisher mutter a cautionary, "Nu-uh."

"Why not?"

He pulled her closer and bowed slightly to be eyelevel. "Because we promised Nora not to cause a scene on her wedding day." He was so close Aiden could feel his moist breath against her lips. Her body responded by moving closer, but he eased out of her reach.

"Fisher..."

"You're still running, Little Fire," he accused, using the nickname he gave her.

"I'm right here, aren't I?" She sniffed, wishing the tears away.

Fisher slid the back of his hand along her cheek, looking more like a caress to the onlookers as he discreetly wiped away a stray tear.

"Yes, you're here, but only partly so. I'm a selfish man. I want all of you. Your fire, your determination, your insecurities, your flaws..." He paused to shake his head in a slow, defeated manner. "I'm tired of only being allowed what you think I'm worthy of having. Aiden, you make me feel unworthy of you. You have no idea how sharp that cuts into me."

Phillip Moreau was a charismatic devil in Aiden's eyes. The man could melt her with lustful longing, yet set a piercing pain to etch wounds along her heart at the same time. She felt unworthy of *him*.

Not being able to stand the conflicting feelings, she wiggled free from his snares and rushed back to the counter with Fisher following right behind her. As soon as her hands landed on the sleek top, she was reminded of the children's game Tag, feeling like she had just procured base. It seemed the estranged pair had made a relationship game out of Tag, chasing each other with abandon until one gave out.

"Let's cut the cake!" boomed a young, familiar voice.

Fisher and Aiden looked over to the DJ's setup and found their buddy, Little J, taking over. They joined the group in a warm chuckle over the young boy's enthusiasm, which was normally quite subdued.

Jernard Ray was new to town. The ten-year-old kid had a heart much brighter than his midnight skin tone. As round as he was tall, it was evident that the "Little" in his nickname was acquired from his short stature. He had perfected the old-man shuffle a good seventy years in advance to needing it. And he talked about as fast as he walked, any slower both actions would be on pause. Nora and Aiden had fallen in love with the cute feller as soon as he waddled into the café several months ago after moving to Florida with his real-estate mogul mom, Sheree.

"We've not eaten the real food yet," someone chided amongst the crowd.

"You heard my friend. Let's cut the cake!" Nora winked at Little J, bringing a big grin to his chubby cheeks, before pulling Levi over to the table where a three-tiered confection was on mouth-watering display.

Once the couple did the customary first cut, a cake server took over and quickly handed out slices of the orange infused treat to the hungry guests. Aiden took a bite, savoring the scrumptious cake, as she watched Nora playfully feed her husband a bite. Levi wasted no time delivering a buttercream kiss to his wife's giggling lips.

"See," Fisher said from behind Aiden, startling her. His long arm reached around her and pointed to the happy newlyweds. "What's so complicated about a wedding that it had you stomping away from ours like a spoiled brat having a temper tantrum?"

The bite of cake felt like it was growing too thick

to swallow from his comment, but Aiden managed somehow to choke it down. The man had an uncanny and completely annoying gift of raising her hackles. Her temper flared at the exact same time the heat lit her cheeks.

Spinning around, she fixed him with a saccharine smile that had him taking a step back. Too much pent-up aggression about their botched wedding fiasco had exceeded its limit. "I can feed you cake," she said through gritted teeth before delivering not just a bite but the entire slice of cake to not only his mouth but also the rest of his unsuspecting face.

Her childish reaction had drawn the attention of everyone in the café, but she was seething and didn't notice. Fisher sucked in a calming breath as he pried a chunk of cake from his cheek. Aiden flinched, thinking the payback was on its way, but he surprised her by cramming it into his mouth and chewing on it thoughtfully. She relaxed her stance and tried pushing an apology out, but he was quicker to the draw and caught her by surprise with the second chunk of cake he wiped off his face. Instead of eating it, Fisher smeared it from her forehead all the way down to her chin.

"Err!" She snarled out a growl while grabbing another piece of cake and plopping it on top of his golden-brown locks. Gasps rang out from the group, but that didn't stop the two from releasing their frustrations with a wedding cake food fight.

Orange and buttery vanilla encircled them as they lost themselves in the escalating argument. In the midst of all the sweet scents perfuming the air, bitter words peppered the situation.

"Can't you let anything go?" he snapped.

"You just always have to keep right on with something!" she snapped back.

"This is all your fault. Not mine!" he yelled.

"Mine? Oh no. This is all on you!" she yelled back.

By the time they were wrestled apart by a few groomsmen, both were covered head to toe in buttercream with their chests heaving.

"Y'all wasting it," Little J whined from his table where he had three cake plates set before him, steady shoveling it in.

"We've been wasting more than cake," Fisher muttered before storming out of the café and seemingly out of Aiden's life.

Chapter Twelve

Silent Treatment Recipe
Begin with one undesired conflict. Stir in overblown proportions of what really happened and a bitter exchange of words until all goes mute.
Recipe Tip: Avoid this recipe. It spoils things terribly and leaves an unpleasant aftertaste.

The heavy sigh escaped the frustrated redhead and joined the ocean breeze. She allowed the ridiculous newspaper to slip out of her grasp, landing beside her chair on the deck. The silly paper had a picture of both her and Fisher covered in wedding cake on the front cover with the caption, Estranged Couple Ruins Wedding. She glanced down at the embarrassment, gave it a good glare, and redirected her focus to the more pleasant view of the beach before her. Spring had finally arrived by the month's account, but good ole Florida had beaten it to the punch a few months back.

Everything was still and seemed to echo the silence that had surrounded her since the epic fail of *not causing a scene* at Nora's wedding last weekend. It had been radio silence from Fisher ever since. He hadn't gone so quiet on her since the debacle of being kicked out of the Sun and Seafood Festival a few years back over an ill-timed food fight gone awry. No texts and no treat deliveries that had become a part of her norm. Several times she'd picked up her phone to message him, and each time she chickened out. Lonely and ashamed of herself, she also considered calling Nora several times to make amends, but didn't want to interrupt the honeymoon. Nora and Levi were on their honeymoon in Nora's hometown in Jamaica and Aiden was terrified they'd decide not to come back.

No Fisher and no Nora. She missed them both terribly. Even Brittany had managed to move away in the last few months to Georgia, chasing after a man of all things. Aiden rolled her eyes at the thought, but stopped, knowing the said man pretty much dragged the blonde beauty away with him. Elliot was a nice enough man, and Brittany was crazy about him. She was just thankful they were in attendance at the wedding.

Still, Aiden was miserable in the lonely state she unwillingly found herself in at the moment. Her silent whines drifted out to the sea, needing some support, but the vivid turquoise water seemed to be paying her no mind at all. It carried on happily while she sat in misery.

I've lost the only man I ever loved.

I won't be surprised if Nora broke her silent treatment only to tell me she was staying in Jamaica to make tropical Cajun babies with Levi.

After showing out at my best friend's wedding, surely

that's what I deserve...

The sound of lazy shuffling drew her attention away from the pity party and over to the side steps, finding Little J waddling up while dragging a canvas bag behind him.

"It's about time you got here. I was about to give up and go home." She stood, leaving the paper alone with her disheartened relationship woes, to meet him at the back door.

"Had to see a man about some shrimp," he drawled, letting himself inside.

Aiden had no doubt who the man in question was with the shrimp. Knowing Fisher was so close, yet so unattainable, made her homesick. She glanced over at Fishermen's Cove. Shaking off the threat of tears, she followed her buddy inside.

The routine since she had met the young boy was he would show up afterschool, which happened to be a little past closing time at the café, wanting to play chef. Aiden and Nora were hesitant at first, but got over that rather quickly when they realized he knew his way around a kitchen considerably well. He'd showed up with a nanny for the first few weeks, but at Aiden's insistence Little J's mom allowed him to be left in the care of the café owners. The kid was probably more mature than most thirty-year-olds in Aiden's opinion.

He untucked his navy polo shirt from his boring khaki pants to get comfortable as he shuffled around the kitchen. Aiden didn't agree with school uniforms. They dulled down children's individualities. Luckily, her buddy was quite a unique individual and the bland uniform did nothing to disguise it.

With great effort, Little J lugged the bag on top of the prep table and climbed up one of the two stools. There he began unloading his tote that was filled with snack-sized bags of odd-looking chips.

Aiden picked one up and examined it. "Hot chili and squid? Where did you get these weird chips?"

Little J grabbed up a bag and opened it before giving it a tentative sniff. "My momma got 'em from a client. They make chips for a living." He pulled out a chip dusted in some green powder and taste-tested it. His flat nose wrinkled, giving away his thoughts. "Don't care for the wasabi and ginger." He offered Aiden the bag but she declined. She grabbed them both a glass of iced water while he looked through the choices.

"Try the squid," she advised, getting a kick out of the "if Mikey likes it, then it's gotta be okay" scene.

Little J took a sip of water and then braved the squid chip. He munched thoughtfully for a few beats and shrugged. "Kinda fishy." He offered Aiden the bag and once again she declined, knowing if he didn't like then she wouldn't either.

Next he popped open a bag of Caribbean jerk flavored chips. When he ate a second one, Aiden figured he found a winner.

"Good?" She asked. This time when he offered she accepted. She gave the chip a lick, taking in the heated flavor that finished on a spicy sweet note. Finding it pleasing enough, she popped it into her mouth. "Hmm... Not bad. I like the hint of cinnamon."

"Yep," is all he said before climbing down to gather various ingredients.

"Whatcha making today?" Aiden watched the kid with curiosity while popping another chip into her mouth.

"Shrimp cakes," he answered while wrestling a jalapeno pepper from the hanging wire basket that was nearly too tall for him to reach. Once he freed one of the green prisoners, Little J grabbed an orange and a red onion. By the time he was done gathering supplies and needed utensils, the prep table was covered.

A few grunts escaped him as he wiggled his way back on top of the stool. From there he set into crushing the bag of chips with his thick fist, dicing the pepper and onion, zesting the orange and tossing it all in a metal bowl. Next, he pulled a bag of plump shrimp from the canvas bag.

"Ooh. Those are gorgeous. You sure you want to risk ruining them with crushed chips? We can grill them instead." Aiden waggled her auburn eyebrows playfully.

"This is serious," he deadpanned, sounding like a wise old man instead of a plump ten-year-old.

"Fine." She sighed and waved for him to continue.

After adding the chopped shrimp to the mix, along with some chopped cilantro and paprika, Little J tossed the mixture with a beaten egg and a dollop of mayonnaise. His chubby hands made slow yet precise work of forming the mixture into patties.

"Are you deep frying or grill top?"

"Grill top with a little bit of olive oil," he directed and Aiden followed his instructions like the good sous-chef she was, heating up the grill and drizzling the surface with oil.

While she grilled the cakes, Little J whipped up a dipping sauce that basically consisted of the juice from the orange mixed with a sweet chili sauce and horseradish.

In no time, they were tearing into the treats with appreciative smacking.

Aiden polished off a third before taking the time to comment. "Okay. We need to order some cases of those chips, so these babies can go on the menu as soon as Nora gets back." *Hopefully, she'll be back.*

"Y'all can't have this one." Little J shook his head before taking another bite.

Aiden dropped her fork. "Why not?"

The recipe had met the criteria for the Orange Blossom Café—yummy and had citrus as an ingredient.

"I already promised it to Mr. Fisher for giving me the shrimp," he answered matter-of-fact.

"What about all *my* stuff you used to make them?" Aiden grouched out.

"You got the last recipe. Both of y'all are my friends. It's not my fault y'all don't know how to behave." His voice remained in a lazy even tone, undeterred by the redhead clearly losing her cool.

"I know how to behave. It's that jerk that doesn't know how." Huffing, she stood and began cleaning up their mess.

"Name calling *ain't* nice, Miss. Aiden," he reprimanded, his southern twang emphasizing his point. Aiden had somewhat of a southern accent, but nothing compared to his South Carolina vernacular. She could listen to the kid talk all day, his lazy tone was so soothing. "You two need to learn to get along," Little J added as he began loading the dishwasher.

Well, maybe not all day long.

She didn't know what to say to that, and was worried the child-man would find a way to get ahold of her again, so she kept her mouth sealed until the kitchen was cleaned.

Little J plucked several cakes off the tray and placed them in a to-go container. He placed it inside his canvas tote before heading to the exit.

"Where are you off to?" Aiden followed.

"Momma is meeting me next door for supper. I want to get Mr. Fisher to try these while they're still warm."

"I feel used, I want you to know!" she hollered.

He didn't pause, simply kept shuffling down the steps of the deck, but fired back, "You ate his shrimp."

She stopped following and let the little rascal leisurely make his getaway.

He's got me there.

Chapter Thirteen

Recipe from One's Past
Take one complicated time in history and add it to a
complicated time of the present. Scoop in surprise and
humiliation to spice things up. Bring to boil until logic is
dissolved into the midst of chaos.
Recipe Tip: Avoid the past at all cost.

The café was bustling with customers, and Aiden
thanked the good Lord that Nora had found it in her
heart to forgive her and come back. The petite woman
walked in earlier that morning and went right back to
doing her thing as though nothing had ever gone
amiss. Aiden knew she needed to take some pointers
in the forgiveness lesson book from Nora and make
amends with a certain frustratingly handsome man.

Vacationers were beginning their holiday earlier
in the season due to a harsh hurricane season
forecasted. Aiden had made amends with Mother
Nature long ago during some nasty seasons, knowing
there was nothing she could do but respect the beasts
that liked to pick on Florida and stay out of their
paths *at all cost.*

While refilling a patron's glass with freshly
brewed tea, Aiden had a sudden bout of déjà vu. A

ghost from her past she had avoided for the last eight years *at all cost* had just appeared in the café, nearly knocking her to the ground. At the moment, she thought the budget should have been increased for this particular beast.

"Not today. Why today?" she muttered, studying the side profile of a dreadfully familiar face. The blond male with well-placed highlights was chatting up a waitress and already had the naïve girl giggling. He was the epitome of pretentious pomp, making Aiden wonder what she ever saw appealing about him. She sat the tea pitcher down on the table, sloshing tea onto her hand. "Excuse me, Mrs. Kennedy."

"Is everything okay," the kind woman asked.

Aiden mumbled a distracted, "Fine," while wiping the tea off with her apron hem and slowly walking over to her dreadful past. She wished she could make him go back there immediately.

Neal turned to deliberately size her up as she marched over to his table. "Wow. Talk about a blast from my past." His voice was too bright and exaggerated, showing Aiden he was just as fake now as he was last time she saw him.

Her memory delivered the unedited scene of him having his way with one of her new waitresses in the back storage room of the café that day. He'd tried lacing his excuse for having the brunette wrapped around him with that bright fakeness. *I can explain, sugar.* She shuddered at the memory and blinked the images away the best she could.

"You're not welcome here," she said in an unnaturally even tone. "I told you the last time you were here to never come back."

"Awe, sugar. You know Aunt Donna wouldn't care for you treating customers this way." He had the audacity to grin.

"Aunt Donna would agree with me that you're not the type of customer approved around here."

"Where is she? Let's ask her." He ran his hand through the short highlighted mane that had begun to recede a bit. That and the few crinkles framing the edges of his blue eyes were the only changes she detected in her ex.

He still sounds like the same obnoxious womanizer, she noted.

Her arms crossed protectively over her chest once she realized his eyes were zeroed in on that part of her. "I guess you didn't stop in at the corner salon yet. If you had, you'd already know Aunt Donna retired several years back and moved up north."

Neal chuckled, finally looking up to meet her guarded hazel eyes. "Didn't she go about that backwards? The south is for retirement."

"What's your purpose here?" Aiden snapped, losing patience with his prattling.

"Mmm... I've missed that husky voice of yours. Come back to my place and I bet I can make it even huskier."

She pointed to the door with a trembling finger. "Out. Now."

Neal mimicked her stiff posture and crossed his

own arms, allowing the fake gentleman frontage to slip completely away. "I'm not leaving."

"The lady says you are," a deep voice said from behind Aiden.

She didn't have to look to know who it belonged to, but wanted to see him too much to not turn around. She found Fisher looming over both her and a sitting Neal. Nora stood by his side in the same protective posture, somehow pulling it off even in her much shorter stature. Aiden's eyes slid back to Fisher once Nora gave her a reassuring nod. With the casual business attire of a white linen shirt and pale-blue slacks, Fisher was obviously working the front of his restaurant next door. He looked intimidating yet way too appealing in Aiden's perspective.

"Just who do you think you are?" Neal stood, but still didn't come close to Fisher's taller height.

"Phillip Moreau. Aiden's fiancé." Both men took a second to glance at her diamond-clad finger for confirmation. "And you are?"

"Neal Denton. Aiden's other fiancé," he shot back, puffing out his chest. Fisher just stood there looking down at him in silence. Thinking he had effectively shut the giant up, Neal's lips began to curve in a smug grin, but his delusional victory was short-lived when Fisher's fist landed squarely with a pronounced whack against his mouth.

Aiden and Nora both gasped in shock at the normally docile fisherman, ignoring the painful moan from Neal as he cupped his mouth.

"That was a friendly tap. I'd be mindful to not ask

me for more if I were you," Fisher warned while dragging the unwelcomed ghost from Aiden's past out the front door by the collar of his pink polo shirt. Once they made it to the sidewalk, he delivered a firm push for emphasis, causing Neal to stumble.

Still holding his lip, Neal spun back around. "This is assault. I'll press charges." His words held a slight lisp produced by the rapid swelling of his bottom lip.

"Awesome. The sheriff is having lunch with my dad as we speak at my place." Fisher nodded his head toward Fishermen's Cove, his golden eyes looking lethal from the severe pinching of his dark eyebrows.

"This isn't over," Neal sputtered, looking behind Fisher to where Aiden stood. He stormed over and loaded up in a fancy sedan before peeling out of the parking space.

They watched on until he was out of sight.

"What on earth was that about?" Aiden eyed Fisher cautiously, not knowing how to react to his violent behavior.

"That was me doing the one thing I've wanted to do ever since I heard that jerk's name for the first time last year. He deserves more than that for what he did to you."

"Violence doesn't fix anything," she muttered, eyeing his red knuckles.

"No, it doesn't, because whatever stupid stunt he did to hurt you way back when has *me* paying the consequences of it now. Really, Aiden, you've let that *nothing* of a man control your decisions all these years? Allowing him to ruin us?" He shook his head bitterly. "Guess I'm not worth it to you to just let him and the baggage he caused go."

Fisher's verbal assault inflicted enough sting to have her flinching away from him just as Neal did only moments ago from his physical assault.

"Phillip…" Before she could say more, he took her hand and pulled her down the alley between their restaurants with hopes of gaining some privacy.

"Why does he think you're his fiancée?" he whispered harshly, plowing his hands aggressively through his hair, causing the brown curls to stand on end.

"Neal said that just to get a rise out of you and it obviously worked," she answered, but he kept looking at her suspiciously. "Tell me you don't believe him!" The humidity pressed against her, adding to the misery of the situation. She hastily wiped the dampness from her forehead, worrying the action probably made her look guilty of something.

Fisher threw his hands up before they landed on his hips. "I don't know what to believe. You made no attempt to deny his claim."

"You didn't give me a chance before punching him!" She began to walk off, but backtracked. "I've not seen Neal since the day I found him having sex with one of my new waitresses in the supply room not even a week before the wedding!"

Her words had them both stunned silent for an agonizing minute.

The sharpness was gone from his tone once he finally spoke, but the words delivered a painful truth.

"See, you're not over that. And I don't even stand a chance because of it. This has gotten out of hand. I just don't know…" He pointed to her finger. "But I think it's best you take that off for the time being."

The pause of her heartbeat before it cracked in agony had Aiden clutching her chest. Somehow, her mangled heart pulled back together and started a staccato rhythm that ricocheted in her ears. The whooshing was so relentless it drowned out the melody of the ocean only a few feet away.

"Okay," Aiden thought she said, but no sound could be detected. Her trembling fingers fumbled with removing the ring, barely able to get it off before holding it out for him.

Fisher shook his head. "Keep it."

"No."

When he continued to refuse it, she dropped it into the pocket of his linen shirt. The tips of her fingers felt the wild hammering of his heart before she removed her hand. A jagged sob broke through, but she quickly swallowed it down.

The burden of what they had just done, severing a promise they made to one another, had them both sagging against opposite walls for support. Holding each other's disappointments within their stares, they remained caught in it for a long spell until the shuffling sound of feet had them blinking the miserable moment away.

"This a bad time?" Little J asked, looking between the two with caution. He was dressed in his school uniform and was holding a folder on top of a clipboard, making him look more like a teacher instead of pupil. His normal Saturday attire was a T-shirt and basketball shorts, but neither Aiden nor Fisher seemed to notice the navy polo shirt and khaki pants.

Without looking away from Aiden, Fisher cleared his throat to rid the emotion and asked, "What's up, Little J?"

Aiden broke the eye contact first, making them redirect their focus to their young buddy. The pair tried slipping into their responsible adult roles, offering up weak smiles with their attention, but from the frown on his wide lips, Little J wasn't buying it one bit.

"I can ask you later..." His short legs began to take a step backwards.

"No, go ahead." Fisher motioned for the young boy to come back.

"Momma talked my school into starting a culinary program, and we're doing a fundraiser to help get it going. Can y'all help out with it?" His normally slow drawl picked up pace, evident he wanted to hurry away from the odd tension between the two restaurant owners as fast as possible.

"Sure," they both muttered while locking reluctant gazes again.

"You just gotta sign my paper." Little J thrust the clipboard into Aiden's hand.

She glanced down long enough to locate the signature line and scribble her name before passing it to Fisher. He did the same and handed it back to the boy.

"Thanks… Well… I guess I'll be going…" Little J hesitated.

"Okay," Aiden mumbled, trying to give him a reassuring smile and failing. She could barely see the boy through the sheet of tears begging to be released.

He let out a long sigh. "I sure wish you two would learn to get along." He began dragging his feet back the way he came, leaving the awkwardness with the guilty parties.

"I wish we could, too," Fisher mumbled, pushing off the alley wall and making for the back door of his restaurant.

Left in the shaded alley, Aiden wilted until landing on her backside. Hidden behind the dumpster, the tears finally broke free, causing her to only feel more trapped in the dreaded past. More tears pushed free when she realized that trap was destroying her future.

Chapter Fourteen

Alternate Recipe for Jealousy
Begin with what you don't have. Mix in a lot of longing for
that particular want. Let it rest until someone else makes a
play for it, then try staking a claim with all of your might.
Recipe Tip: Gather all the fact ingredients first to prevent
making a fool of yourself.

One month passed, bringing the end of May along with it. The heat and tourism had both kicked up a scorching notch during the raucous month of unwanted advances and ridiculous rumors. Aiden had her hands full trying to keep Neal out of her frizzy hair and hushing the buzzing from the busy-bees of the community. The gossipers were quick to spread it around that her ex was in town for business for the next month. The grapevine also said he was considering staying permanently if Aiden would give him a second chance.

Frustrated at that prospect, she tried pushing her hand through her hair, but the tangle of curls caught her fingers in its snares.

"Err!" Pulling the mass of hair over her shoulder to get a better look at the frizz, Aiden cringed with knowing she needed a salon visit, but that was a dangerous endeavor with the rumors swirling around. Those stinking rumors danced through her thoughts as she studied her dead ends.

Aiden O'Connell was caught with her ex-fiancé in a compromising situation by her estranged fiancé. Twenty witnesses knew there was nothing compromising about the exchange at the café until Fisher delivered that punch.

Prominent restaurateur Phillip Moreau spent the night in jail on assault charges. The town knew too easily how to perform their daily mugshot search on the internet and knew good and well Fisher's handsome face had not made an appearance.

Aiden is pregnant and doesn't know who the father is. She was still a bit scrawny from the wedding crash diet for goodness' sake.

Staring at her dark auburn hair, she muttered, "Just need more frizz-control conditioner... Or maybe move to a less humid place far from here."

Leaving the hairy situation alone, Aiden turned back to the computer screen just as Nora cleared her throat, making the redhead jump and clutch her chest. Turning, she found her friend standing in the office doorway with a look of disdain pinching her elegant features.

"Ya not leaving me with this mess, so buy some more conditioner." The petite woman waved a fistful of papers in the air.

Aiden rolled her eyes. "Talk about me being a bit dramatic. It's just papers for crying out loud."

"Do ya know what these papers say?"

Aiden shook her head and offered an uncommitted shrug with really not being in the mood for the guessing game.

"Ya better start caring." Nora handed over the paper in a flourish of exasperation.

"What is this?" She shuffled through the papers, but Nora pulled the orange flier to the top and tapped it.

"From what I gather, ya one of the chefs being auctioned off for a dinner date."

"Why would I do that? You're the chef around here. Not me. Besides, I never agreed to this." Her feistiness overruled the passiveness she'd been trying to pull off as she waved the papers in the air.

"Apparently ya did. It's to help raise money for the culinary arts program at Little J's school."

Aiden blinked. Then blinked again as it dawned on her. "Ohh... That little devil didn't mention anything about me having to be auctioned off." The papers floated to the desk top before her forehead joined in a loud thump.

"Speaking of the devil, he's in the kitchen experimenting with a new recipe."

Aiden was out of the chair and marching to the kitchen before Nora could continue. She halted at the door when a foul smell hit her nose, causing her friend to bump into her back. Nora steadied herself and took a step to stand beside her friend. Aiden glanced at the young chef to gage the situation, not wanting to chance insulting his cooking skills. He kept wrinkling his flat nose every so often, so she knew he found the odor coming from the dish offensive, too.

Sidetracked by the odd odor, she forgot about the auction momentarily. "Whatcha got there?" she asked cautiously.

Little J shrugged. "It's supposed to be a recipe for the summer cooking course. I can teach it to the class if the teacher approves, but... this project is going sideways." He mixed the concoction with a grimace on his face.

"Sideways? Closer to upside down and round and round."

He looked up with a grave expression. "This is serious."

"Speaking of serious, what's up with you auctioning me off?"

He shuffled the dish to the trash bin and tossed the brown contents with disgust. "You agreed to help my school's fundraiser."

"You didn't think a better explanation as to what I was agreeing to would be helpful?"

"You were kinda busy that day..." Little J avoided her and Nora's scowl as he headed to the sink to scrub the dish past clean.

"I don't think this is a good idea." Aiden crossed her arms and leaned against the sink while Little J rewashed the dish for good measure.

"I agree. Sardines are unredeemable." He dried his hands after releasing the sink water.

"You are correct about sardines, but you know that's not what I was referring to."

He glanced up at her and softened his brown eyes, pulling on the puppy dog expression proven to help him get his way. "Please."

Aiden looked over at Nora. Her friend grinned way too mockingly. She stuck her tongue out at Aiden and wandered into the dining area of the café.

"You know Nora is the chef around here. Why didn't you ask her instead?"

Little J glanced around to make sure Nora was out of earshot and whispered, "She's kinda boring. Momma said we'd make a killing, if I got you and Mr. Fisher instead of your chefs since the town really likes talking about you two. And y'all always in the paper for something or the other."

Aiden rubbed her forehead and groaned at all the truth the adolescent Yoda just delivered. "Sheree ain't a self-made millionaire for nothing."

Little J nodded in agreement. His mom's success was always being highlighted in various entrepreneur magazines.

"And she said she would match whatever the school raises." He scooted closer to Aiden and looked up with those sweet brown eyes. "So can't you and Mr. Fisher maybe show out somehow this week? What about a prank? That would be awesome."

"Now you're pushing it, you little punk. Put those puppy dog eyes away. It's not working this time." Aiden averted her eyes and scooted out of the kitchen before his little look-weapon reeled her in against her will.

~ ☼ ~ ○ ~ ☼ ~

"This is really pushing it," Aiden grumbled while the stylist tried pinning a wayward curl back. She was still taken aback that the fundraising event came equipped with wardrobe, hair, and makeup stylists. She could hear Little J's words echo in her head.

This is serious.

"Sorry," the young woman named Jill said when the bobby pin dug into the redhead's scalp, causing her to wince. "If you would just stay still…"

Aiden brushed the woman's busy hands away and put a few steps between them. "This is as good as it's going to get." She leveled a look at Jill when she began to lunge at her with another bobby pin, so the stylist relented and turned to inspect the owner of the sweets shop.

"Are you sure I can't talk you into the other outfit?" a prissy guy from wardrobe asked for the hundredth time.

"No," Aiden replied for the hundredth time. "I already told you, an orange bikini is not an outfit." She tried fixing him with a glare but her twitchy eye made it nearly impossible. Pressing a finger to the jumpy nerve, she hurried away before he made a lunge at her, too.

Music with heavy bass began to pulse through the sound system out front, sounding more like a dance party than a school fundraiser. Aiden's heart racked up its tempo along with the music when people began rushing about in a frenzy behind the curtain. Not knowing what to do, she just stood there until someone grabbed her arm and steered her to line up behind a few other women. Looking around, she nervously searched for any glimpse of Fisher, but he was being sequestered with the other male chefs in a classroom.

"Ladies first," is what the fundraiser coordinator explained earlier when the five women began to nag him on why the men weren't being put through the styling ringer along with them.

Shaking off her annoyance, Aiden focused on the MC's voice on the other side of the curtain as she welcomed everyone and explained the night's events. Aiden adjusted the hem of her coral miniskirt that barely peeked out from the edge of the chef's jacket. She had to give it to them, the white jacket with her café's logo and her name embroidered on the lapel would be a great keepsake from the night's embarrassment.

An assistant ushered the owner of the bakeshop to the stage, causing the large gathering to break out in applause.

"Ladies and gentlemen, help me welcome our first chef, Miss Kristen Lane." More applause. "She is the fine owner of Memory Lane Bakeshop. Her hobbies are…"

Aiden tuned the MC out and rolled her eyes heavily at her line buddy, Shayna. "Is this a flipping beauty pageant?"

Shayna finger-combed her brown bob down, and was rewarded with a death glare from Jill. Shayna eyed her back and continued to tame her mane down a few more inches. She snorted when the hairstylist broke eye contact first. Shayna turned her attention to Aiden's question. "Sounds like it. With this big hair and thick makeup, it feels like it, too." She exaggerated a cringe.

"Bad childhood memory?" Aiden asked, already knowing the answer.

Shayna Clary was the reigning queen of every festival back in the day. The leggy brunette rebelled against her mom's dream of her becoming Miss Florida and on to Miss America by tossing her crown aside and pulling on an apron to make all the treats she had been denied while having to fit into the formfitting gowns and swimsuits all of her teenage years. The woman could make a sinful caramel. Her decadent establishment sat across the street from the café and was rightfully named Sinfully Sweet. Aiden couldn't ask for a better neighbor.

"Let's start the bidding at five...hundred dollars," the MC drawled out.

"What's a fair price for an auctioned-off chef?" Aiden wondered out loud, thinking five hundred was a hefty price tag.

"That price best get up to at least a few thousand or I'm refusing the date," the scantily clad owner of the all-natural vegan restaurant hissed from behind them. The raven beauty looked close to a vampire with her milky white skin and scarlet-red bikini. Yes, she was the only one to agree to the swimsuit outfit.

Aiden couldn't help but be impressed by the

wardrobe stylist for talking the unnaturally gorgeous woman into such attire. She averted her eyes to the tiny black chef's coat with the red logo to Venus's stitched sideways on the open lapel.

"Honey, you've managed to make the least appealing type of food sexy. You deserve a few thousand," Shayna offered, openly appraising the boldness of Venus's outfit.

Venus's expression turned smug. "I know." *And so sure of herself...*

"Eight-fifty?" the MC questioned. "Anyone? Remember, this is for the children."

"Nine hundred," someone shouted out, earning a few gasps and applause.

The chefs all murmured their awe over the high bid, while Venus sniffed unimpressed. Moments later the red-faced bakeshop owner hurried off the stage to meet her date and the MC announced the next victim. This continued until it was Aiden's turn. Most went for close to a thousand, so her goal was set there with hopes of contributing around that amount. She made it to the stage under the glaring lights as the MC began the weird pageant spiel.

Having enough of the theatrics, Aiden stepped over to the podium and snatched the microphone from its stand. The MC's eyes rounded in disapproval, but the redhead ignored her. If she was going to put up with a bunch of boloney, then it surely would be on her own terms.

Sashaying to the center of the elaborately decorated stage that was way too sparkly for her taste, Aiden raised the mic to her sassy lips. "Y'all know who I am," she assured them with as much bravado as she could muster. "I'm the co-owner of the tastiest place on this here coast!"

Shouts and whistles came heavily from Nora's table, where their wait staff and friends were gathered.

Aiden grinned at them before continuing. "Knock, Knock."

"Who's there?" the audience chanted back, readily playing along.

"Orange," she exaggerated out.

"Orange who?" they shouted.

She propped a hand on her hip, producing her finest faux-beauty-queen stance and said, "Orange you ready to start bidding?"

A roar of laughter danced along the guests as she waited for the first bid.

"Six hundred," Nora shouted.

"That's a good starting point," Aiden commented, looking around for the next bid.

"Six-fifty," some young guy offered near the front.

Aiden looked down where he sat in front of her and shook her head and winked. "Sweetie, don't embarrass me with that tiny bid."

"Eight hundred," he challenged back, dark-blue eyes trained on the prize.

"Better—"

"Two thousand," an all-too-familiar voice called out from the back of the room, freezing out any fun

Aiden had been having at the expense of the cute guy.

Neal stood up, making sure everyone knew it was him proposing the bold bid. Arms crossed and smiling way to smug.

"Twenty-two!" Nora screeched out.

Without taking his eyes off Aiden, Neal countered, "Twenty-four."

"Twenty-six," called out a raspy voice from the right side of the room.

Aiden tore her glare away from her ex to search out the bidder, finding a grey-haired man smiling back. "I think we have a winner!" she rushed to say, wanting to end it while Neal wasn't ahead.

"Twenty-eight!" Neal yelled.

"Three thousand," the old man countered.

"Done!" Aiden exclaimed, hurrying off the stage.

The older man stood as she neared and outstretched his arms for a hug. Aiden decided three grand earned him a hug, but quickly jumped back when she felt a sharp sting on her backside.

"You just pinch me?"

"I figured you owed me that much." His bushy eyebrows waggled around in defiance.

"Well, consider us even, so you better keep those hands to yourself." She popped his hand and narrowed her eyes to drive home the warning.

The crowd chuckled and that's when Aiden realized she still held the mic. Face in flames, she turned to find an annoyed MC with her hand held out.

After snatching the mic back, the woman

stomped to the stage and faked a laugh. "And that, ladies and gentlemen, is the one and only Aiden O'Connell." She placed the mic in its designated holder on the podium and got back to business. "Okay, I do believe we've got one more lady chef to auction off. Help me welcome to the stage Venus!"

Aiden snorted, thinking how Venus dropped her last name several years ago like she was Madonna or something. She turned her attention from the stage and handed the old man a card that was placed in her coat pocket to hand out to the winning bidder with the date information on it and hurried over to Nora and the crowd to take in the rest of the show.

Venus strutted out full of confidence while the same young guy who bid on Aiden joined in with his friends in shouting out with catcalls and whistles. The vixen played it up for them, earning her bids to top out at two grand. Frowning, the beauty slung the date card on the guy's table and stormed out, but not before sending Aiden a glare.

"I can't believe ya out-did that one." Nora laughed. "And by the geriatric section at dat!"

The table laughed along and Aiden shrugged with indifference.

"It's all for the children." She batted her false eyelashes at her friends, playing it up while secretly thanking her lucky stars the old man beat out Neal. She stubbornly kept her eyes averted from the spot he had been standing, wishing he would disappear back to wherever he had been for the last several years. No matter where she went in the last few weeks, he somehow managed to be there, which was beginning to creep her out.

The tempo of the music changed to a sultrier pace and the lights dimmed even more, effectively creating a more seductive atmosphere.

"What is this? From pageantry to strip club?" Shayna asked from the table adjacent from Aiden's. She shoved another bite of cake into her mouth while glancing toward the stage and almost choked on it. "Oh my word!"

All eyes followed Shayna's and found the chef from the BBQ joint just inland taking his place on stage. He wore a chef's jacket over his jean overalls. No shirt.

"For a BBQ hillbilly, that Wyatt is *hawt*!" Shayna slapped the table and shouted out, "One thousand!"

Wyatt confidently stood on the stage, smoothing down his long black beard that actually touched his bare chest. He winked in Shayna's direction, sending the women in the audience into a tizzy.

"Good grief," Aiden muttered as the ruckus began to escalate.

"Take that chef's coat off and I'll bid twelve hundred!" a woman shouted from up front.

Squeals and giggles bounced around when his jacket hit the stage while Wyatt slowly strutted in a circle to display the backside of his attire, showing off the ink whirling around his well-defined shoulders and upper arms.

"Those overalls don't do a thing for his butt!" Aiden directed her comment to Shayna as the brunette bounced in her chair.

"Fifteen hundred," Shayna called out before looking over at Aiden. "Looks like a present needing to be unwrapped if you ask me."

Wyatt upped his game by pulling his thick mop of dark hair out of the more hip than hillbilly man bun. This sent the female crowd into a wild frenzy of bidding.

Aiden threw her hands up. "Okay! Wyatt is *hawt*!"

"Two thousand!" Shayna nearly growled the bid while sending a warning glare out to any female daring to bid against her. She didn't wait for any response before walking boldly to the stage and pulling on the discarded chef's coat. "Let's go, big guy."

Grinning behind the monster of a beard, Wyatt grabbed Shayna up and easily slung her over his shoulder. He marched off the stage and right on out the back entrance.

"Wow. Wyatt is like a hillbilly caveman." Nora fanned her faced.

"I can carry you around, woman, if that's what it takes to get you all hot and bothered." Levi gave his flustered wife a sly look.

"Later," she said, causing the table to break out in a rumble of laughter.

A few more men made their sexy way around the stage while women bid on them like rabid old maids. Aiden sat tight, knowing the best was being held for last, and that would be none other than Phillip

Moreau with his sunshine and surf charisma.

The atmosphere seemed to be closing in on a crescendo when the newest restaurateur on the block strutted onto stage. Marx Crass with his black rimmed glasses and pale lavender mohawk had a mysterious air about him that paired incredibly well with his gastro pub named The Mad Chef. The bids began before the MC could finish her information spiel.

"Venus should have stuck around. I think Marx could compliment her dark and eerie rather well," joked one of their friends.

Aiden couldn't help but smile, remembering how Marx seemed to sneak in town overnight a few months back and set up a Tim Burton themed pub that advertised molecular gastronomy mumbo jumbo and served his drinks in beakers. Fisher had teased Aiden about her turf being was once again threatened.

"Maybe you should leak all of the liquid nitrogen out into his indoor garden," he taunted, reminding her of all the pranks she had pulled on him when he arrived unwelcomed on her *turf*.

She missed his teasing. His flirting. His bickering with her. She just missed the aggravating man. Period. She barely noticed when Marx exited the stage to deliver his card to an older lady with bright-magenta hair.

Dropping her chin onto her palm, Aiden sighed heavily and tried to keep her cool as Justin Timberlake's "Can't Stop the Feeling" began to pump through the speakers. Her breathing halted altogether when Fisher strutted out onto the stage.

"Oh my word! Can ya believe he agreed to wear that?" Nora shouted over the screams.

All Aiden could do was shake her head in shock. She watched as Fisher flashed his heartbreaking smile, lighting up the stage. Her eyes left the megawatt grin and traveled to the yellow fishing bib he wore underneath the grey, unbuttoned chef's coat. The suspenders hung lose along his hips instead of clinging to his bare shoulders.

"Were they giving out spray tans backstage, Aiden?" their friend Jess asked.

Aiden, unable to peel her eyes away from Fisher's nicely bronzed form, could only shake her head.

"Nah. Dat's from last week's fishing trip with our buddy Charlie." Levi sounded right amused by the girls' banter over his friend and boat mate.

Ah, Charlie... The notorious childhood friend of both Levi and Fisher. Fisher's dad had described to Aiden once that the three of them were considered the trouble-making trio of their parish back in Louisiana as teens. She felt slightly comforted that Fisher had his friends to lean on during these last few weeks. Nothing seemed to relax that man as much as fishing. Too bad Aiden had found nothing to aid in her comfort, mainly due to her blaming herself for making such a hot mess out of their beautiful relationship.

Fisher gave the audience a cheeky grin as he peeled off the fishing cap and tossed it at them, looking like a flirty pro. He raised both arms and ran his fingers through his unruly locks, effectively flashing more of his bare chest.

"You think they oiled him up? It's hard to tell from here!" another friend asked, slapping the table and howling like a wild hyena. "I knew we should have sat up front!"

The MC volleyed tidbits of Fisher's Q&A between screams and squeals. "When asked how he keeps life spicy, Phillip Moreau says all he needs is a little fire to keep his life interesting."

Aiden's eyes met his in a flash. Even with the distance between them, there was no mistaking the pointed look he gave her. Little Fire is what he called her, saying the meaning of her name fit her to a T. Her heart fluttered in her throat, causing her mouth to go dry. Nora reached over and squeezed her clenched fist.

Fisher looked away first, going back into Magic Mike character with shucking off the chef's coat and tossing it to the stage, giving the audience a better view of his exposed chest.

"Let's start the bidding at one thousand," the MC demanded, knowing with certainty Fisher was about to make the most bank for the fundraiser.

"The man looks like a watersports catalog model for goodness' sake!" exclaimed one of the café waitresses.

The entire situation felt too much like a meat market in Aiden's opinion, and from the look on the prime beefcake's face, he felt the same way. Once the bidding was underway, Fisher's confident demeanor declined to uncertainty. His golden eyes darted around, looking lost and anxious all of a sudden. He kept studying the room, not finding whatever or whoever he was searching for.

"Not sure if I agree to this circus, but you've gotta give it to the school for coming up with it." Nora shook her head.

"Ain't that the truth? No bake sale would have come close to, what, twenty grand so far?" Brittany asked. She made a special trip home just for the fundraiser.

As the bids hit twelve hundred, an exuberant shout from the back of the room offered, "Three grand."

Gasps followed the audience's attention to the daring bidder, finding a shockingly gorgeous blonde rushing through the doors.

Aiden glanced back at Fisher, thinking he'd be even more uncomfortable, but her stomach plummeted when she discovered him in quite the opposite state. There he stood in the center of the stage, hands perched on his lean hips with a grin splitting that handsome face.

"Thirty-one hundred," a cougar with unnaturally orange hair shouted. She sat at a table near the middle of the room with a half dozen more women looking similar to her. Their hairdos were so loud each head practically glowed in the dimly lit place.

Fisher's brows lifted at the hot blonde, clearly challenging her to bid again.

"Four grand!" she counteroffered with no hesitation.

"Forty-five," the cougar yelled, earning her high-fives from her brightly styled entourage.

Fisher nodded to the blonde and winked and Aiden caught all this on the verge of tears.

"Six grand," blondie replied, earning another approving wink from Aiden's sun deity.

Sadly, at the moment, all of his warmth was directed away from her and it left Aiden feeling dark inside.

What have I done? The question had plagued her like a nagging bad dream in the last few weeks. The man on that stage wanted her as his permanent partner in life and she'd gone and ruined it with her bullheadedness.

Heart pounding and eyes stinging, Aiden's gut instinct screamed at her to storm the stage and lay claim to what was rightfully hers, but she remained glued to the chair. Stubborn to a fault.

The cougar tried fruitlessly with bidding only a puny fifty more dollars with the blonde coming back with seven grand. This effectively concluded the bidding war. The blonde shimmied around in a little dance of victory with fists pumping the air.

"Who is that?" Aiden asked no one in particular. *And why does she have to be so blame gorgeous?*

"Dat's Charlie," Levi answered before hurrying over to where the stranger stood.

"Charlie?" Aiden muttered and then repeated the name several times in her head. *Charlie? This is* the

Charlie? The same Charlie the guys meet up with a few times a year for fishing trips?

Aiden leaned close to Nora and whispered, "How has it gotten past us that their fishing buddy is very beautiful and very much *female*?"

"Ya didn't know?" Nora asked back, sounding guilty of something.

Before Aiden could find out, Levi came back to the table with Charlie under his arm. "You saved our boy in the nick of time."

"No doubt. I got stuck in Tampa traffic. That punk is lucky I didn't get a ticket or he'd be forking that out of his pocket, too." Charlie's voice was just as appealing as her looks. It was mellow with lilts of creole hitting certain syllables.

"Can't believe he just bought himself for seven grand." Levi laughed with the blonde joining in.

Charlie's sparkling blue eyes skipped around the table, taking in everyone's inquisitive faces, hesitating at Aiden with a dubious look, before popping Levi in the stomach with a good bit of force. "Stop being rude, will ya, and introduce me to your friends."

Before he could comply, Fisher stalked over and grabbed Charlie up in a bear hug, lifting her athletic frame right off the floor. "I was about to panic, you little twerp!"

Charlie whacked him in the arm. "Put me down. You're getting me all oiled up."

Aiden's breath seized in her lungs when he deliberately rubbed himself against the blonde to deliver more oil off his chest and onto her thin tank top. Charlie squealed and slapped at him.

Raina, one of the waitresses leaned close to Aiden's ear. "So they did oil him up. *Dang...*"

Aiden could only nod, unable to look away from the set of sturdy arms holding the stranger. The very set that should have only been allowed to hold her that way. *I've done this to myself.*

Levi snorted. "You two bicker like an old married couple."

Nora's green eyes dashed to meet Aiden's to assess how she was holding up. The edges of those sharp peeps softened when she saw the good amount of hurt the situation was inflicting on her friend. Without a word, she began gathering Aiden's belongings along with her own, clearly about to stage a rescue dash. Before she could get Aiden out of the chair, Fisher delivered enough bite to have Aiden limping in pain for weeks.

"Maybe I should marry this ole gal. Charlie definitely knows how to be committed to someone. She's loyal like a boss, and ain't ever let me down."

Aiden finally unglued from the chair and was out the door just before the tears spilled. A roar of laughter from their table followed her out into the sultry night. Inhaling the thick briny air relieved some of the pressure building in her chest. Yanking off her sandals, she picked up her pace and made a run for it.

Chapter Fifteen

Recipe for Awkwardness
Set yourself apart from the crowd and mix in
uncomfortable glances from them. Add an additional set of
guests that stir the whispers around you. Ignore the
embarrassment profusely in hopes it will go away.
Recipe Tip: Careful not to allow this recipe to come to a
raging boil in front of said crowd. More awkwardness is
sure to follow.

Inspiration was exactly what Aiden needed to get over the awkwardness from last night's debacle of a fundraiser, so she scurried out of bed Sunday morning and set out on her bike to the café just before worship service was to begin on the beach. Beach towel and travel mug of coffee in hand, she took a deep breath of the briny air and allowed the warm sand to tickle her bare feet. She kept her sight on the rolling waves and let the group gathering around Preacher Jeff to blur, but the murmurings picked up as she set her towel down and plopped on top of it. Not being able to ignore the chatter, she glanced around and froze on a set of golden irises.

Why me? What have I done to deserve this?

"Mornin'," Fisher greeted from the towel right next to hers. Charlie sat beside him, sending a menacing scowl in Aiden's direction. Both were casually dressed in shorts and tank tops, but looked like they could be a Greek god and goddess relaxing on the sand, glowing in their bronzed glory.

Unable to find her voice, Aiden nodded and looked toward the preacher. She tried composing her face to a casual expression, but her entire body itched with wanting to bolt off the towel and run away. Aiden felt so transparent in the early morning sun with too many eyes scrutinizing her.

Turn around. Nothing to see here! She wanted to scream this to the nosy ones craning the necks to get a peek, but offered them a wobbly smile she couldn't steady no matter how hard she willed it.

Please don't fall apart in front of this crowd. Hold it together, girl. Hold. It. Together! She chanted this to herself, but the burning in her throat that threatened to produce tears indicated the pep talk was failing miserably.

"Glad you folks joined me this fine morning. God has placed on my heart to share with you about commitment. Turn in your Bibles to…"

The rustling of thin paper carried along the breeze, but there was no denying the heavy snort that came from Fisher's towel companion. Aiden's eyes betrayed her by looking over at Charlie to see what the snort was about. She found the blonde looking directly at her. The hurt and humiliation began to turn into a rancid anger.

Aiden narrowed her own gaze. *Who do you think you are?* Making sure to convey to the blonde that her little show was not going to intimidate her, Aiden stared for a solid measure before slowly looking away.

Preacher Jeff spoke for the next thirty or so minutes about how the Bible defined commitment, but Aiden had the hardest time following along. She was close to reaching her boiling point with Fisher's little friend. Charlie snorted and huffed and shouted several amens directly towards Aiden throughout the service, efficiently drawing too much attention. No doubt, it was her intention.

Closing prayer seemed the perfect time to sneak away from the tension, but Aiden sat still for a change.

I'm so tired of running.

It was obvious that blondie had something to get off her huffing chest, so Aiden stayed firm on her towel until everyone had wandered away for the rest of their Sunday. Not surprisingly, Charlie dawdled around, too.

"Come on, Charlie." Fisher nodded for her to follow, taking a few steps toward his restaurant deck in hopes she'd follow. No such luck.

"She obviously has something she needs to say," Aiden said, not taking her eyes off of Charlie. She sized the woman up, finding a few inches in height difference and maybe a little more muscle in favor of the blonde. The shorts and tank top showed off an impressively toned physique. Athletic for sure, reminding Aiden of a small tidbit she remembered about Charlie. A professional beach volleyball player.

She'd always pictured a bronzed male when Fisher spoke of Charlie.

Boy was I wrong.

"Spit it out already." Aiden crossed her arms and jutted out her chin.

"You deserve to have your butt handed to you." Charlie stabbed her finger at Fisher while glaring at Aiden. "That man is made out of the finest cloth, and you were stupid enough to just throw him away like he was nothing more than a rag." She took a step closer, looking down her nose at the redhead with the anger rippling off her body.

"Charlie," Fisher said in a sharp reprimand. He gave Aiden no time to rebuke or agree to the statement, grabbing Charlie by the upper arm and practically dragging her off the beach.

The flush warmed along Aiden's neck and on toward her face as she watched them disappear inside Fisher's restaurant. Tears stung her eyes, but she refused them freedom. Sniffing them back, she forgot about her bike and began the trek back to her apartment on foot.

Monday. A start of a new week was exactly what Aiden thought she needed. That was until most of the café's customers came in to check on her, hearing that Charlie had taken a swing at her after yesterday's worship service.

"This town is starting to close in on me. I'm thinking the idea of packing a bag and disappearing into the night is sounding rather appealing." She slumped in her chair while ignoring the bubbly surroundings of Sinfully Sweet.

"So dramatic," Nora chided before taking a sip of her latte.

Both women had gravitated across the street after closing to find something sweet and caffeinated to perk their spirits after the hectic workday.

"I don't see any black eyes, so hold your head up, girl." Shayna walked by and placed a caramel brownie beside each coffee cup. Patting Aiden on the shoulder, she hurried back to the kitchen, leaving a delicious aroma whirling around their table.

"Everyone thinks I've been fist-fighting over a boy." She groaned and slumped down even further.

"Maybe you should. Then, at least, the poor guy would know you truly care." Nora narrowed her eyes, daring Aiden to refute her words.

Aiden chose to roll her eyes and leave the words off the table. Humiliating flashes of Fisher's public dis at the fundraiser, Charlie's bold threat, and Nora's brutal comment had Aiden's mouth puckering. She took a long sip of the caramel latte, begging the sweet liquid to cleanse the offensive taste from her pallet. The sip hadn't slipped completely down her throat before her mouth grew rancid again due to the scene across the street. She looked toward Fishermen's Cove at the exact same time Fisher came barreling out the front door with a laughing Charlie clinging to his back like a monkey. He playfully dumped the blonde in the passenger's side of her red convertible sports car and hopped into the driver's seat.

"Does she not own anything else to wear besides

bikini tops and cutoff jean shorts?" Aiden pushed the untouched brownie away. She smoothed the front of her stained and slightly frumpy T-shirt, feeling right down on herself.

"Oh no. Don't go lettin' that mind of yours deliver a pity party. No comparing ya self with anyone but ya self."

Too late. Aiden chose to simply nod while keeping her gaze froze on the vivacious couple outside.

Both women watched on as the blonde practically launched herself in Fisher's lap and began tickling him as he mussed her hair. The realization hit Aiden that where she had failed at making him happy, Charlie had succeeded. He seemed to be handling their broken engagement rather well, but it left Aiden feeling half-dead. The distress had stolen her appetite and another five pounds from her body.

Finally, Fisher pushed the grinning woman from his lap and took off down the road. A wave of jealousy squeezed at Aiden's stomach so severe it forced her arms to hug her abdomen.

Swallowing past the lump in her throat, she whispered, "Charlie's right. Fisher is made of the finest cloth, and I've ruined everything... I'm so stupid."

Nora clucked her tongue in a prudish manner before turning away from the window. Eyeing Aiden in disdain, she muttered, "Pity party, pity party. Self-depreciation is such an unappealing characteristic."

Aiden pounded her fist on the table, sending a splash of coffee from both cups to hit the table. "Can't you give me some advice instead of being snarky with me?"

"Dawg nyam ya suppa." Nora took a dainty bite of her brownie while Aiden huffed at the Jamaican saying that Nora seemed to favor when it came to the redhead.

"So this is what I deserve? These are my consequences for what?" She waved her hand at the road where the shiny car had just zoomed down.

"Ya let a mistake of ya past manipulate every decision ya make now. Even letting it run off an exceptional gift." The Caribbean lilt hit each of Nora's words, which was always more pronounced when frustrated.

"What gift?"

Finally, a subtle look of pity crossed Nora's delicate features. "*Love.*"

Swallowing proved to be difficult once again for Aiden. She glanced down at her hands resting on top of the table. "Gosh, I miss him."

"Then ya need to let him know that before it's too late." Nora reached over and grasped Aiden's forearm, giving it a reassuring squeeze before releasing it.

Aiden rose from the table as Nora's phone dinged. "You're right."

Nora checked the text as she asked, "Where ya off to?"

"To track down my blunder and make it right."

"You'll have to wait about a week before ya can make it right. Levi just text that they've pulled out of the marina."

"Another fishing trip?" Aiden glanced back at her friend.

Nora nodded. "Yeah."

"Wow. That was a quick getaway."

"Maybe ya not da only one running from a broken heart." Nora gave Aiden a pointed look, answering, but not answering directly, that Fisher was suffering as well. She had made it clear from the get-go that she wouldn't discuss anything Levi shared about his best buddy with Aiden.

Aiden returned to her chair in defeat. "Why's she even here? The past two years have practically been Charlie-free. Why now?" She heaved a frustrated sigh. "She didn't even show for your wedding. How's that being a loyal friend to Levi?"

"Charlie is a pro volleyball player. She was actually training for the Olympics until a shoulder injury a few months back. The poor thing was in the midst of surgery and rehab during the wedding. So enough with ya whining about da girl."

"You're actually taking up for her?" Aiden jutted out her chin and looked more like a bratty child than the lethal redhead she was aiming to achieve.

"So I should be mad at Fisher's lifelong friend for taking up for him and trying to be there for him through a difficult time in his life?" Her delicate brows shot up.

Having enough of Nora's blunt lip, Aiden threw a few bills on the table and marched toward the exit.

"Dat's right. Keep on running from da mess ya

made."

The sting of Nora's words made Aiden's pace quicken. Opening the door, the humidity rippled over her like an unwelcomed hot flash. She headed for the comforting shade of the palm trees lining the sidewalk until the breeze of the ocean called her in that direction. Plopping down in the sand, she spotted a boat disappearing over the horizon. Not wanting to think about the woman on that boat who was taking her place, Aiden forced her thoughts to a happier place.

Just a week before Fisher's romantic gesture with the surprise wedding, she was by his side on another boat.

~ ~ ~ ~ ~

Phillip Moreau looked just as at home on the sailboat as he did on his commercial fishing boat. Sure, him dressed in his casual linen suits welcoming guests to his restaurant suited him just fine. But the freedom of the open sea lit the man up, proving him rightfully at home there.

As he captained the sailboat, Aiden watched his every move in pure admiration. With the sun glinting off his bronzed skin and the relaxed smile gracing his handsome face, she was completely captured by his enigmatic lure.

"I love you," she blurted, causing his smile to ease into a spectacular grin. The man practically sparkled.

"And I love you, Little Fire."

The day was spent with Fisher at the helm and Aiden trying to stay out of his way. He warned her it would be a long trip out to sea, but she didn't care. Having him all to herself was a rare treat with them both busy with their businesses and the small coastal community making it their business of keeping tabs on the spunky couple.

Somehow, the day drifted by and was replaced by a clear night where the stars kissed the edge of the ocean.

"Lay back and enjoy the stars, woman." Fisher pulled Aiden to her feet and guided her to the bow of the boat where he quickly made a makeshift bed with several colorful pillows and a few beach towels. With a wave of his hand, he directed her to lie down.

Snuggling amongst the pillows, Aiden found herself surrounded by the brilliance of the night sky twinkling from all sides. "This is what God had to have intended for our lives. Not the hustle-and-bustle madness we've created." She sighed with contentment as she watched Fisher maneuver the boat along the water with such confident grace.

"You're absolutely right. And boy did He make a masterpiece out here for us to admire." His eyes scanned the open ocean with such admiration.

Stretching in the fashion of a lazy cat, Aiden couldn't contain the smile making her cheeks ache. It had been plastered there ever since Fisher had showed up at her door at four that morning to steal her away. The only thing she could think of that would make her happier was if he was lazing beside her. "Why don't you drop anchor and join me?"

"Soon."

Not much later he did just that, but didn't join her. Patting the spot beside her, Aiden encouraged him. Shaking his head slowly, Fisher's boyish charm danced along his wide grin and sparkled through his golden gaze as he offered his hand. Without question, she took it and stood. The expression on his face was enough to make her pause and appreciate it by running her palm along his scruffy cheek.

"You have a secret you want to share with me?" Anticipation tightened her belly.

The man didn't disappoint. With a nod of his head toward the water, Aiden's attention turned there, first in confusion and then in pure awe.

A surprised gasp escaped her lips as she hurried closer to the side of the boat to get a better look. The water was glowing in vibrant bursts of neon blues and greens. It reminded her of twinkling Christmas lights.

"What is that?" Aiden muttered the question, but was unable to look away from the spectacular phenomenon to seek Fisher's answer.

"Water fairies," he whispered close to her ear, the warmth of his breath sending a tingle along her neck in the process.

If she closed off the cynical rationality of her adult brain and basked in a naïve flash of childhood innocence, Aiden could clearly see the sparkling fairies dancing just under the surface of the calm water.

"Seriously, what is it?" Her eyes darted to his, but quickly returned to the radiant show.

"My momma said they were water fairies and that's what I'm sticking with. Come on now. Don't spoil the magic of it."

Aiden had no power to deny his request. He was absolutely right. *Why ruin the magic?*

"Tell me how y'all came to meet these fairies?"

Fisher draped an arm over Aiden's shoulder and drew her closer. "My dad took us out on a fishing trip before I was even tall enough to see over the side of the boat. That night while Momma spread out a picnic to keep my sister and me occupied, Dad brought us here." He looked out over the twinkling show with a far-off gaze. "It was the most magical night of my life. Peering over the side of the boat while standing on a bucket, my parents shared their water fairies with us for the first time. After that, we made it a Moreau tradition of coming out here once a year to visit the fairies."

They remained quiet for a spell until Aiden asked, "You went without me last year?" She looked over at him, trying not to feel disappointed.

Fisher shook his head. His smile wavered slightly, but he managed to keep it in place. "This is the first time I've come for a visit since Momma passed... Dad and Madilyn went last year, but I just wasn't ready."

"Phillip..." Tears filled Aiden eyes, blurring the water fairies.

He placed his fingertips under her chin and tilted her head upward. "I'm ready now. I consider you a

Moreau already, so I wanted to share this family tradition with you." He paused to skim his fingers along her cheeks. "Aiden, I cannot wait to share the fairies with our children."

"Me too." Leaning up, Aiden pressed a kiss to her magical deity's warm lips, feeling beyond blessed to be able to call him her fiancé. The tender kiss wandered down a lazy path of caresses, but increased in momentum, leaving them both breathless.

With his hands tangled in her wild curls, Fisher froze suddenly and pulled away from her lips. His head angled sideways with a sparkle of mischief in his eyes. "You hear that, Little Fire?"

Aiden mimicked the angle of his head, trying to catch whatever noise drew his attention, but found nothing but the lulling ocean lapping against the boat. "What?"

"It's the fairies..." Fisher cocked his head even further and grinned. "They want us to take a swim with them."

"What? No." Aiden shook her head hesitantly. Her focus volleyed between the vivid scene dancing on the water and Fisher. "Is it safe?"

Apprehension and curiosity warred against each other, but Phillip Moreau had come to know his Little Fire all too well in the last two years. The satisfying look he gave her proved he already knew she would join him. As he offered his hand, Aiden granted fear a break that night and accepted his challenge. Taking a deep breath, she allowed him to pull her to the edge of the boat where they leapt into the dark water.

Wherever they caused a splash, the glow would ripple out, beckoning the ocean to sparkle in vivid blue and green bursts.

Giggling, she blurted, "You're magic!" She ran her fingers through his wet hair, sleeking it away from his forehead.

Fisher held onto her as he spun them in a circle with the majestic sea and night sky suspending them in the enchanting moment. "Don't you think it's time we make some magic together?"

Aiden pressed her palms to his chest where the rapid beat of his heart met her touch. "Are you propositioning me, sir?" Her eyes narrowed.

"No. I already did that last year and you agreed by accepting my ring. You're mine, and it's time to make that a permanent title." He kicked his feet to spin them once again. "Baby, we needed to be married like yesterday."

"Fisher..."

"I need to start each day with you in my arms and end each day the same way." His paused to clear the emotion from his throat. "I need to make love to you. To create babies from our love..."

With the night so flawless and magical, Aiden could see the future Fisher presented, so clear it was as though she were looking at it through glass.

~☼~☼~☼~

Shame clamped down on Aiden as the memory of that beautiful night faded back to the harsh reality.

"My life has run amuck at no fault but my own,"

she muttered toward the receding tide, wishing it would take her blunder out to sea with it. Her hasty blunder reminded her of how quickly a storm could come up out of nowhere and wreak havoc on a beautiful day. Feeling no better about anything, Aiden rose and dusted the damp sand off before heading home.

Chapter Sixteen

Fearful Recipe
Begin with a solid portion of a possibility and stir in a scoop of the unknown. Allow several what-ifs and uncontrollable factors to add a sharp bite to the flavor. Stew on it until fear becomes debilitating and ruins all measures of joy.
Recipe Tip: It's best to focus on truths instead of what-ifs.

"Storm's coming in, so I'm only making half da baked goods today." Nora mixed orange muffin batter while her eyes kept flickering to the kitchen windows.

No evidence of a storm could be found on the sunny beach just outside, except for the aggression of the waves rolling in with a bit more force than usual.

"Okay," Aiden muttered as she prepared to brew some tea.

The café was abuzz with the patrons chatting up about the tropical storm that had spontaneously formed just off the coast overnight. The tourists hightailed it as soon as it was announced, but the locals didn't allow the threat to bother them too much. It reminded her of the verse from 2 Timothy that Preacher Jeff shared Sunday.

For God hath not given us the spirit of fear; but of power, and of love, and of a sound mind.

The week in Fisher's absence, Aiden had spent the time trying to work through her reaction to the surprise wedding.

Was it my stubbornness?

Was it his spontaneity that threw me for such a shocked loop?

Her effort to figure it out had felt pointless until the church service. God made it perfectly clear what the problem had been. As soon as the preacher read 2 Timothy 1:7, she knew.

Fear.

I'm downright scared, is all there is to it.

She was scared of the what-ifs, the uncontrollable factors that come along with such a great commitment, and of being hurt again. All of which was not fair to Fisher.

She had yet to lay eyes on him. And truth be known, she was still wrestling with fear of how it would turn out when she finally did see him.

The morning progressed as did the evidence of the storm. With the winds picking up and the dark bands charging towards the shore, the locals finally decided to head home to prepare. After finishing up the cleaning of the dining area, Aiden sent the waitresses home. She pushed the mop bucket to the kitchen where Nora was packaging up the unsold baked goods.

"We need to call Sheree to make sure Little J ain't gonna try venturing out to play Top Chef today."

Nora glanced up from the white pastry box. "She already called. Poor kid has da Chickenpox."

Aiden wedged the mop in the corner for later. "Really? Who gets the Chickenpox during summer break?"

"Little J obviously." Nora shrugged. "I'd bring him these goodies, but I've never had da chickenpox."

"No worries. I have, so I'll run them over." Aiden hung her apron on the wall hook. She couldn't help but ask, "Does Fisher know he's sick?"

"Probably. They were hanging out yesterday when Little J started running a fever."

The ache of wanting to see Fisher hit her hard. Breathing through it, she grabbed the box. "Okay. I know he'd want to know."

Nora rested her hand on top of Aiden's arm. "Yes. And I think Fisher would want to know how much ya missing him. What happened to ya telling him before it's too late?"

"I'm... I'm working it out." Aiden didn't wait for a reply as she scurried out the door. Manning her bike she maneuvered the short trek over to Little J's house.

The visit was short, but quite lively. A wired-up Little J was in rare form due to having an adverse effect from the Benadryl he was taking to combat the itch. By the time Aiden made it back to the café, she was actually tired from trying to keep up with the edgy chatterbox.

Nora walked into the kitchen and found Aiden chugging a glass of water. "What happened to ya?"

"Little J wore me out." She panted between gulps.

"Our Little J?" Nora eyed her.

"Yes. The kid and antihistamines don't get along. He was bouncing off the walls."

Nora chuckled. "Now dat's one of those things I'd have to see to believe." She thought about it for a second and shook her head. "I can't even picture it."

Aiden hitched her thumb towards the front of the café. "Go ahead. Levi is outside waiting on you."

"Where are ya staying?"

Aiden reached around the wall and switched dining area lights off. "Here, probably. I've got to work on the books anyway. Now's the perfect time to catch up on paperwork."

"Nonsense. Come home with me or go over to Fisher's place."

"No—"

"Aiden, ya my dearest friend. I love ya, but ya getting on my last nerve!" Nora picked up her purse and slung it over her shoulder.

"Aren't you a peach? Thanks." Aiden hurried to her office, wanting to get away from the tongue lashing following hot on her heels.

"This is like one of those dumb romance novels where da main characters can't get their heads out of their behinds long enough to see what they have." Nora slapped the doorframe, causing her frustration to echo down the hall. "Enough with da drama. Everyone's tired of it. Time to grow up and fix da mess ya made!"

Nora wasn't the type to leave things on a bad note, but proved she was completely at her wits end by storming out. As the door slammed, Aiden sank in her chair. Angry and humiliated, she felt like a child after a scolding.

Nora had been on a repeat lately, not allowing Aiden a chance to forget who was to blame.

Not Neal.

Not Fisher.

Aiden. It was all on Aiden for tarnishing her relationship with Fisher.

She remained slumped behind her desk until footsteps sounded down the hallway. She hurried out of her office and almost ran into a figure in the darkness.

"Aiden, it's just me," Neal said, grabbing her fists before they collided with him.

"And that makes this better how?" she barely asked over a husky whisper. She yanked her hands free and took a step back. "Why are you here?"

"Why do you think?" He gestured toward her.

"Sorry. I've already sent all the waitresses home. And the storage room remains locked nowadays."

Neal snorted and shook his head. "You need to get over that."

Aiden shoved him with all her might, catching him off guard and causing him to stumble a step. "Get. Out. Now."

"Will you knock it off," he demanded, but didn't bother fighting against her.

She kept pushing until they reached the back deck, but he quickly spun around and had her pinned against the building in a flash.

"Stop fighting it, Aiden. You win. I've learned my lesson. It's time we give this another chance."

"No. I have Fisher." She struggled to get around him, but Neal kept her pinned.

He snorted again. "Looks like the hot blonde has him. Time for you to wake up, sweetheart."

"No. He's mine." She growled while wrestling.

Neal refused to release his hold on her. Instead, he leaned in and fixed his lips to hers. He tried forcing her lips to part, so she did the only thing she could think to do.

She bit the tar out of him.

"Ow!" He dropped his arms and dabbed at his bottom lip. He pulled his hand back to inspect it, but found no evidence of blood. "You bit me."

"Yeah. And if you ever try that stunt again, I'll be sure to draw blood next time." Aiden shoved him for good measure. "I don't love you. I never loved you. I had familiarity and love confused back then. I didn't know what the word truly meant until I met Fisher. I'm in love with him. Yes, I've screwed that up. You can relate."

Throwing his hands up in the air, Neal began stomping down the deck stairs. "Fine. Stay alone. I give up."

Aiden did something her stubborn side would normally refuse. She allowed him to have the last word, hoping by staying mute he would hold good to his promise and keep walking away. The dark clouds rolling in caught her attention. She closed her eyes and inhaled the suddenly cooler air.

Unbeknownst to Aiden, Fisher stood next door on his deck, catching the entire exchange between her and Neal.

When she opened her eyes, Fisher was before her. His gold eyes gave her a once-over before pulling her close. As his arms engulfed her, it began to rain in earnest. Aiden felt him walking her backwards inside, but kept her face buried in his shirt. She dared not look up for fear he'd disappear and take his warmth with him.

Once inside, he leaned away. "You okay?"

"Yes," she whispered.

Fisher dropped to his knees in front of her and began kissing languid paths up her right arm, and then repeating the same to her left. The blood roaring in her ears blocked out the torrential rainstorm as her trembling body swayed in the darkened kitchen.

"What are you doing?"

He murmured his answer along her tingling skin. "Erasing that man's touch from your skin." He stood back up and claimed her lips, saying against them, "Mine."

His touch was almost fevered, but she felt the same way. Aiden allowed him to kiss the sunshine back into her as the storm began to pound the shore just outside. The skies were dark and mournful, but all she felt was the warmth of happiness. As they pressed closely, confusion and then reality reared their ugly head.

Breaking the kiss, she stated the sad truth, "But we're not even together anymore."

"That stupidity has gone on long enough."

"I thought you were done with me." Needing a break from his intense gaze, she turned her head and stared at the stove.

Fisher followed her eyes. "You think our feelings for each other can be switched off as easily as that six-burner Wolf stove?" This grabbed her attention back to him. He shook his head. "No. There's no off switch to this love. You're foolish to ever think that."

"But—"

"Yes, I hit a pause with us, hoping your stubborn little behind would work out whatever issues you have. Our love is here, but like any dish left too long on a burner unattended, it's gonna get ruined. We're close to that now and I just can't allow that to happen." Fisher leaned in and kicked up the flame setting with a white-hot kiss, completely scorching Aiden. She latched on to him and met his caress with her own scolding amount of fervor.

The lightening flashed and the thunder clapped as the tropical storm slung a rain band onto shore, but the couple was oblivious to it.

"If you were only my wife…" Fisher trailed a hot path down her neck with his lips, releasing a guttural sound when reaching her collarbone. "I want to claim you completely."

A stuttered laugh slipped from Aiden's lips as she laced her fingers through his thick locks. "You just want me to say 'I do' so I'll have sex with you."

His head shot up to glare at her. The intensity made her body shiver. "Go ahead and put that sarcasm away, Little Fire. This isn't the time for it." Fisher inhaled sharply, holding the air inside him before pushing it out. "Yes, I want you. I want a lot of things. I want to show you how much I'm in love with you. I want to celebrate that love properly in our marriage bed."

The sincerity of his words left her unraveled and raw with emotion. Tears began tracking down her face.

Fisher wiped them away with the back of his fingers. "Baby, I'm not a patient man. Never claimed to be, and you've tested it like no other." He placed his lips against her forehead and held her for the longest time. "I'm not pushing your hand like I tried last time, but I'll be next door when you're ready to head on over to the courthouse."

This made her snicker. "During a tropical storm? I don't think so."

He reluctantly let go and walked to the door. "Like I said, I'll be next door, so hurry up."

Aiden shook her head, thinking the bad weather must be the cause for the bizarre behavior she had witnessed—Little J acting hyper, Nora being uncharacteristically cold and prickly, Neal trying to rekindle something from only ashes, and Fisher coming behind him to scald her with his alpha male performance.

Luckily, the storm showed itself fickle, leaving as fast as it showed up. Within a few hours the only signs of its visit were scattered palm fronds and loose garbage. As the sun righted itself in the sky, Aiden wandered out of the office where she had made no headway with the thick stack of paperwork. Too much was on her mind to concentrate. She moved over to the front of the café to peek between the blinds to see if Fisher's truck was still parked outside. Yes, it was there, but the red sports car parked beside it made an itchy heat crawl along her neck.

Having enough, Aiden spun around and rushed out the backway and continued in a clipped pace until she reached Fisher's kitchen. A few kitchen workers and the chef were going over menu specials when she burst through the back door.

"Umm... Hey guys. Where's Fisher?" She fidgeted from one foot to the other.

The chef looked toward the front before looking back to Aiden. "He just left."

Aiden took off to the front, passing through the empty dining room, but halted once she had the front door halfway open. She peered out through the opening just in time to see Charlie driving away with Fisher in the passenger's seat of her car.

"Well, I guess your patience ran out." Not wanting to face the curious eyes back in the kitchen, Aiden left through the front.

As she locked up the café and headed home, the defeated redhead couldn't help but agree with Nora completely. She was living out some silly scene in a cliché romance novel. She felt the stinging blow of rejection, the dizziness of passion, and a bitter taste of angst all within a few short chapters of her life.

ORANGE BLOSSOM CAFE

Chapter Seventeen

Recipe for Rumors
Take one snippet of the truth and toss in several offhanded remarks. Mix until an entirely new and distorted version is formed.
Recipe Tip: This recipe never turns out the same way twice. Variations will surely occur.

Aiden stood at a precipice, willing herself to be brave. *Run or take it like a woman?* This particular undertaking had already been put it off way too long, so taking it like a woman seemed to be the only option. Nora finally put her foot down and went behind the frizzy redhead's back and made her a hair appointment. It had been two excruciating days after the epically disappointing reconciliation with Fisher. Rumors had been set off in a tailspin about the love triangle—*Fisher was seen at the café with Aiden... Fisher was seen leaving out of Fishermen's Cove with his arm around Charlie... Fisher ran off to marry Charlie*—but Nora told her to pull up her big girl panties and carry on.

"That's it. I'm going in." Aiden hitched her baggy jeans up on her hips, imagining them to be her big girl panties as Nora had put it. As the door jingled a warning of her arrival, several curler-covered heads and tin-foiled heads bobbed in her direction. "Hello, ladies." Aiden barely held back the cringe after hearing the fakeness in her own voice. After taking a cleansing breath that did no good due to it being laced with strong chemicals, she stepped over to the check-in counter. The group of women had grown unbearably quiet. Only a blow dryer dared to make a peep from one of the back stations.

"Nelly will be your stylist. She'll be right with you," the receptionist said as she looked Aiden over in blatant scrutiny.

Hitching her jeans back up onto her hips, Aiden nodded and proceeded to shuffle over to the waiting area, but before she could take a seat someone called out her name. Glancing up, she noticed a black haired woman with bright blue eyes looking in her direction. The stylist smiled and waved her over.

A trip to the shampoo station held precedence when the first thing Nelly did was get her fingers caught in the tangled snares.

"That won't do." The stylist tsked as she worked thick globs of a heavy-duty conditioning treatment through Aiden's hair. "You spend a lot of time on the beach, don't ya?"

"Yep," Aiden muttered, not feeling up to taking offense. Truthfully, most of her time was at the café, which left not much time for spa treatments. Especially when she had been avoiding them for almost a year. The hens normally gathered here and boy did they like to cluck about her and Fisher. Sure, they were gathered today, but were keeping the clucking to a whisper. There was no denying the pressure of their inquisitive gazes on her.

The stylist massaged her scalp with no rush, causing Aiden's eyes to grow heavy. *Maybe Nora was right. I've been too dramatic about this public appearance, too.*

As she relaxed, her guard decided to ease down. By the time the conditioner was rinsed and Aiden was directed to the stylist's chair her guard had completely left the building.

"Okay. What would you like done, besides me hacking away a foot of dead ends?"

Aiden's eyes snapped up to the mirror, but relaxed slightly when the stylist winked back at her playfully. "Honestly, I don't care. Just don't give me a buzz cut."

"Okay, hon." Nelly patted her shoulder before grabbing the shears.

Aiden thought if the woman got scissor-happy at least she wouldn't have to make another appointment until next summer. Before Nelly took the first snip, movement caught the corner of her eye. Being careful not to move her head, she looked over to the right and then to the left. The hens had descended. A flock of curlers and tinfoil scooted too close for comfort on various rolling chairs—some rolled to a spot with a backwards scoot, some took the side shuffle, while others did an awkward inchworm. They were blocking any chance of escape. Aiden couldn't stifle the eye roll.

Here we go...

"You ladies may want to shuffle back. Nelly is about to whack into this fuzz." She watched with hope, but the warning fell on deaf ears. It seemed her engaging with them only brought the flock closer.

"You've got a gorgeous head of hair. It just needs some taming... and shaping up... and curl serum." Nelly nodded her assessment and made the first snip.

Aiden eyed her audience. *What do you ole bats want?*

It's as if one of the purple-haired curlers read her mind. "Seems your Phillip had a sleepover last night." Ms. Tierney sniffed self-righteously while smoothing down her smock.

"He's not *her* Phillip anymore," Ms. Gladys piped in.

"Well, good riddance. Aiden, that man is a bit too loose for my likings. You're better off without him." Ms. Rosette clucked her tongue with the rest of the hens echoing her sentiments.

"I agree. Fast women in fast cars spending the night at his place." Ms. Nelson shook her tinfoil-wrapped head.

"How do y'all know all this?" Aiden spit the question out before she could swallow it back down.

The hens looked over their shoulders in what seemed to be a synchronize routine before leaning closer to Aiden. She noticed each one had snippets of dark-red hair gathering in their laps. *That's what they get for meddling.*

"Janice Schumacher lives next door to Phillip. She

said that red car didn't leave until late this morning." Ms. Tierney sniffed again. "Stayed in the same spot for *two* days."

"Loose, I say. Too loose." Ms. Rosette narrowed her eyes behind her bifocals.

Aiden nodded once Nelly put the scissors down. She begged the stinging in her eyes not to produce any tears. She wondered if his declaration had turned out to be as fast and fickle as that tropical storm.

The stylist must have sensed the tension mounting Aiden's shoulders. She spun the chair and yelled over her shoulder for the other stylists to gather their wandering clients.

Once the squeaking of the rolling chairs disappeared, Aiden muttered a quiet, "Thank you." Nelly patted her shoulder in reply and went back to cutting.

After a session with the blow dryer, Nelly turned the chair back to face the mirror. "You look fabulous."

Her hands went to test the bouncy curls framing her face, discovering them to be baby soft. She looked over her shoulder and noticed most of the long length remained.

"I layered it so the curls wouldn't be so heavy." Nelly grinned as she admired her work.

After settling the bill and leaving Nelly a generous tip, Aiden hurried out of the salon without making any eye contact. Their whispering clucks followed her until the door shut. What irked the young woman the most is *why* gossip in the first place? What did the gossipers really gain from spreading rumors?

Chagrinned, Aiden laid on her couch the rest of the afternoon, running her fingers through her ultra-soft hair to soothe the overwhelming hurt of the hens' words. The phone rang, pulling her out of the comatose state. She didn't recognize the number, but hesitantly answered it anyway.

"Hello?"

"Aiden, dear, this is Ms. Gladys."

Aiden sat up. "Oh. Can I help you?"

"I thought you'd want to know... Janice just called and said the red car is back again." She tsked loudly into the phone.

The phone call had just been enough to send the irritating spot of hurt into a full-blown outbreak of anger. Aiden saw red. "You listen real close, lady. Just because I visited the salon doesn't mean I signed up to be a part of you hens' busy-body club." Aiden heard Gladys gasp, but she plowed on. "Please remove me from your gossip phone tree, and learn how to mind your own business!" She hung up and plopped back down on the couch, the air leaving her in a heavy whoosh.

It took only ten minutes of stewing before Aiden was climbing in her Prius and heading down the path that lead to Fisher's house. It was time to face the chaos head-on. As she pulled up, she noticed there was no sign of the red car. Undeterred, she hurried up to the walkway and banged on his door.

No answer.

Not letting that stop the mission, Aiden swiped

the hideaway key from the ledge of the doorframe and let herself in. She was met by silence with only a subtle hum of the air conditioner in the background. Thinking no one was home, she began to back out but stopped at the sound of a moan coming from Fisher's bedroom. She marched over and began banging on it.

"Fisher! Open this door!"

"Go away!" he yelled through the door.

His response, both harsh and unexpected, doused Aiden like acid.

"No!" Open this door and face me!" She jiggled the doorknob and found it locked.

"Give me a minute. I'm naked!"

That response was also unexpected and nearly pulled a sob out, but she took a shaky inhale to force it back down. She slammed her fist against the door. "Tell Charlie to get dressed, too, so I can kick her butt!"

The doorknob came to life on the other end and then the door opened swiftly, sending it against the bedroom wall in a furious slap.

Aiden stilled when her bleary eyes landed on Fisher's broad bare chest. The only thing he wore was a pair of pajama bottoms slung dangerously low on his hips. A lot of bronzed skin was exposed and was riddled with red dots.

A snort and then a snicker escalated into a full-scale fit of laughter.

"It ain't funny," he gritted out.

"Yes. No! You're right." Aiden snorted. "So not funny." She had to cover her mouth with her hand when his glare heated.

"Just leave," Fisher mumbled, scratching at his neck with a gloved hand.

"Why are you wearing gloves?"

"So I won't gouge chunks out of my skin." His deep groan echoed throughout the entire house as he commenced to scratching his backside with no regard to his company.

"You just scratched your hiney in front of me!" Aiden couldn't stifle the giggle. Poor guy had to be miserable, but he was so darn cute at the moment with his curls sticking out all sorts of ways and his skin covered in dots.

He looked at her in pure misery. "Just be glad it was my *hiney*, 'cause there are other parts needing a scratch, too." He began to squirm and released a mean growl.

"You poor thing. You are eat up."

"Yes. They're *everywhere*," he grumbled.

"What are you doing for the itch?" She took a step forward to inspect a spot on his shoulder that looked to have been recently scratched to the point of drawing blood.

Fisher flinched back. "I'm contagious."

"I had Chickenpox in middle school. I'm safe." She glanced down to where he was rubbing his toes along the top of his opposite foot and repeated, "What are you doing to help with the itch?"

"Charlie got me some pink junk, but it's no good."

The smile Aiden was fighting fled at the mention

of that name. "Why didn't you call me?" There was no disguising the displeasure in her voice.

"Charlie stopped by after the storm passed through. That's when I noticed the fever. By the time she got me home I was covered in this crap." He motioned at his red splattered chest. Even his handsome face and earlobes were speckled. "I didn't know if you'd had them before or not. She had, so she volunteered to take care of me, but I kicked her out today. Worse nurse ever," he grumbled as his hand inched closer to his groin.

"Stop scratching or you'll have scars," Aiden warned. She had a feeling he wouldn't get over the virus without a few reminders left along his skin. She had never seen such a bad case as his.

"I can't," Fisher said, giving in and scratching right in front of her, releasing a satisfied moan.

Aiden averted her eyes and took in the ocean glistening in the late sun just outside his sliding glass doors. "Go take a swim. The salty water should calm it while I go the pharmacy."

"You think it'll help?"

Aiden shrugged. "It makes sense… It won't hurt to try."

Fisher's large form hurried past her, clearly on a mission to find a solution to combat the itch. Aiden caught a glimpse of his polka dotted backside as he stripped with abandon and dove into the waves.

"Good thing this is a private beach!" she hollered out once he resurfaced.

Fisher acknowledged her by throwing a hand up

before disappearing again under another wave. She left him to it and headed out.

Forty minutes later, after phoning Little J's mom and a nurse she knew for some Chickenpox treatment pointers and a trip to the pharmacy, Aiden arrived back to Fisher's beachside bungalow. She found him sitting chin-deep in the ocean.

"Hey," she called out as she made it to the shoreline with a towel.

Fisher glared over his shoulder. "I about decided you weren't coming back."

"Aren't you in a mood? I've got supplies to help with the itch." She dropped the towel and started to backtrack to the house.

"You're leaving?" The panic in his voice had her turning around.

"No. Just giving you some privacy."

"I wouldn't need any if you were already my wife like you should be. Heck, I don't mind now." Even though the last part could be categorized as flirting, his sharp delivery said otherwise. He began to stand with no care about flashing her, but Aiden spun around and rushed inside.

Moments later, Fisher joined her in the kitchen with the towel secured around his waist. She thrust a few pills into his palm. "Benadryl and Tylenol," she explained while holding out a glass of water. "I've also run you an oatmeal bath."

He studied her before running his fingers through the soft red curls framing her face. "I love your new hairdo." Even in the midst of his sick misery, Fisher noticed.

"Thanks. I had to endure the gossiping hens to get it, though."

Fisher looked as though he wanted to say something. Instead, he nodded and made his way to the bathroom. "Please stay," he said over his shoulder.

"I'm not joining you in the bathroom," she tried teasing, but it fell flat. Clearly, he wasn't in the mood.

He frowned at her while scratching the side of his head. "Just don't leave. *Please*." He stood on the threshold of the bathroom, looking miserable and lonely. It was exactly how she had felt for the last two months.

"I'm not leaving you," Aiden whispered, meaning much more than just the moment they were suspended in.

Fisher understood and exhaled the breath he had been holding. "Thank you," he whispered back before closing the door behind him.

Aiden eased over and sat against the door. She heard splashing and then a deep groan as he settled into the tub.

"Don't turn the jets on. The oatmeal would probably clog them."

"It smells like breakfast in here," he called out. A second later she heard him spitting.

"Don't put it in your mouth!" she ordered sternly.

"It sure doesn't taste like breakfast," he grouched out.

"Are you hungry?" She didn't even think about

feeding him. Her mind was focused on finding him relief from the rash. "I can make you something."

"Later. Just stay right there for now. I missed your voice."

Aiden smiled and settled against the door. "I missed you, too. Think I made that perfectly clear earlier."

"That was pretty sexy how you charged in." Again with the flirting, but delivered in a grouchy tone.

Aiden deduced it to how miserable he was with the rash covering him from head to toe. She shook her head at her brazen entrance earlier. "I guess I owe you an apology for that."

"No. It showed me you really do care."

"I've never shown indifference when it comes to you, Phillip. That should be enough testament on how much I care about you."

"Your spunk is one of the things I love most about you, Little Fire." The sound of water sloshing onto the floor reached Aiden where she sat by the door. "How much longer do I need to sit in this stuff?"

Aiden glanced at her watch. "About ten more minutes."

Fisher groaned and more water splashed around as he must have settled back into the tub. "I don't even know where I got this cursed virus from."

"I thought you knew Little J was sick."

"With a cold."

"*No*. He has Chickenpox, too. But nothing like

your case. Just a handful of dots."

"He's dead to me." He sniffed loudly, sounding like a mob boss.

"That's a bit dramatic, don't you think?" She couldn't help but smile over his animated declaration.

"He gets just a few of these little devils, but I get millions?" he yelled, sounding like he slapped the water in the process.

Aiden snickered. "You have hands-down the worst outbreak I have ever seen. And that's saying a lot. I witnessed the entire sixth grade at my school come down with it. Even my teacher and the art teacher were speckled."

Fisher released a long moan.

"Stop scratching!" she shouted at the door.

"It's all over my scalp, too!" he shouted back. More splashing echoed from the bathroom, probably from him dunking his head into the oatmeal bath. Then some more splashing. "This is sending me to the grave." He went back to moaning.

"I want my ring back!" Aiden blurted, trying to distract him from his scratching frenzy.

It worked, too. Water sloshing and then wet footsteps rushed to the door before he yanked it open, sending Aiden backwards. She looked up and found him looking down at her. Thankfully, he'd grabbed a towel first.

"You really want to marry me?" he asked slowly, doubt infused each word.

"Why else would I have said yes that day on the dock when you asked?" She took his offered hand

and allowed him to pull her to standing.

"To pacify me?" He shrugged his wet shoulders.

Aiden looked him square in the eyes, not wanting him to miss her sincerity. "I said yes one time in my life that I regret. I knew the moment I agreed to marry Neal it was a mistake. It felt wrong. But I knew before you asked me, I was supposed to marry you one day. It felt right." She rested her palm against his speckled cheek. "The only mistake I've made with you is letting my fears and stubbornness get between us. I shouldn't have run away from our wedding. It's my biggest regret."

They stood there with Fisher riddled in red polka dots and dripping wet while a sniffling Aiden clung to him.

After a few more minutes of holding each other, Fisher let go and disappeared into his bedroom. He reemerged wearing a pair of loose boxers. The ring box in his hand.

"Don't ever take it back off," he demanded in a soft voice, melting Aiden's insides as he pulled the ring from the velvet box and slipped it back onto her rightful finger.

"Promise."

"Please don't ever run again." Tears swam in the golden depths of his eyes.

"I can't promise that." Aiden placed her finger over his mouth before he could grumble. "But I can promise to bring you with me."

She stood on her tiptoes and kissed him until she hoped he'd forgotten about the rash and her blunder altogether.

Chapter Eighteen

Recipe for A Happily Ever After
Take one independent heroine and add one handsome alpha
hero. Mix in a conflict, a dash of an obstacle, and allow the
trouble to stir. Next, add a healthy serving of clarity to
resolve any angst. Finish with the anticipated kiss, the
tender caress, two rapid heartbeats, and combine into an
awe-inspiring conclusion.
Recipe Tip: Don't use Aiden and Fisher as an example on
how to get your happily ever after!

With the ocean breeze beckoning, Aiden walked with a determined pace onto the beach. With no walls to hold back their praise, the seaside worship service seemed livelier than normal. She paused and watched on as the sun finally woke up and began warming the surface of the teal water in hues of glittering orange and pink. She caught sight of her sun deity at that moment and grinned. There were no doubts that the day was going to be exquisite.

"Welcome to another day the Lord has made. Before we get too settled, how about we welcome one another." Preacher Jeff waved his hand out in encouragement.

The guitars strummed quietly, serenading the

gathering as they began moving around. Aiden walked over to greet a friend but her attention remained fixated on Fisher. He stood tall and proud with a devilish smile on his face. An elderly lady ambled over to him, but he kept his focus on Aiden as he offered the woman a hug. Once he was free, he began to dodge through the crowd, but Aiden made a path directly to him. She kept hot on his heels while divvying out some welcome hugs along the way.

Fisher graciously spoke to each person he passed as his stride quickened, but her goal to catch him never wavered. Aiden continued to shoot warning glares each time he peeked over his shoulder at her. He, in return, widened his grin and accepted her warning as a challenge instead.

Only a few minutes eased by, but it felt like an eternity to her, as she helplessly watched Fisher expand the distance between them. The two of them were playing some sluggish game of chase, and she knew for certain she was not going to lose. Fisher lingered at the front of the group and spoke to Preacher Jeff. Aiden took advantage and plowed right into his awaiting set of outstretched arms.

Pulling him flush against her body, Aiden murmured in his ear, "Tag, you're it."

His rich chuckle gave away to just how pleased he was by her game. "No, Little Fire. I let you catch me, now I'm gonna let you keep me."

Aiden turned her attention to their preacher. "Say, Preacher Jeff, you feel like having a wedding today?"

A murmur broke out through the group as all eyes focused on the couple standing up front.

"This is serious," Little J drawled out as he waddled over and stood beside Fisher. "I'm the best man."

Aiden and Fisher looked down at him and chuckled. Their little buddy was sporting a bowtie for the occasion. The sneaky little kid found Aiden icing her wedding cake the day before, but promised not to say a word. He told her he was just glad her and Mr. Fisher were finally behaving.

"Dat it is, my fine fellow," Levi spoke as he walked up with a tiny silver tray holding the wedding rings in his hands. "I'm the ring man."

"*Bearer*," Little J corrected.

"Nah. I'm a *man*." Levi grinned as he joined them.

Nora walked up next with flowers in her hands. "And I'm da flower *woman* and da matron of honor." She handed Aiden a simple yet elegant bundle of orange blossoms.

"Looks like we've got everything we need." Fisher grinned down at his bride. She wore a simple white sundress that reached her bare feet. He looked equally as nice and stylish in a pair of tan linen pants and a white linen shirt. His feet bare as well.

"Y'all ain't fooling anyone!" Ms. Tierney sniffed loudly as though the whole situation was foul. The couple looked in her direction.

"She's right." Ms. Nelson nodded in agreement. "The two of you are *already* married."

"You dragged that poor man as sick as he was to

the courthouse two weeks ago. Shame on you for having him out and about with Chickenpox," Ms. Rosette chimed in.

Aiden laughed. "You're defending my husband today? You were just calling him too loose *two weeks ago*."

Fisher's brows pinched together as he looked down at Aiden. "She called me *loose*?"

Aiden nodded in amusement. "You ladies don't normally attend these services. What are y'all doing here today? And how on earth do you know we're married?"

"Janice Schumacher said she saw you two at the courthouse signing the marriage license. You're supposed to sign it *after* the wedding." Gladys tsked, acting like she'd caught them red-handed of some ludicrous crime.

"And Janice also said she saw your family leaving out of Fisher's house this morning." Ms. Nelson pointed over at Aiden's parents who flew in from Ireland. Aunt Donna stood with them as well as Fisher's dad, sister, and Charlie. "She thought y'all might have something planned."

"I think we need to move," Aiden muttered to Fisher.

"No, but we're installing a privacy fence after the honeymoon." Fisher drew her closer.

"I've been enjoying this extended honeymoon." She smiled up at him. "And I can't wait for the next leg of it."

The hens were still clucking, but the couple had

tuned them out. Not Little J. He huffed out a breath of frustration before slowly spinning around to face them.

"Y'all ladies are being rude." His chubby hands planted themselves on his hips. "And I ain't havin' it. My friends want to celebrate. They even got us cake and some other food. Now, y'all either pipe down or you can leave." He raised one hand and pointed toward the alley between the restaurant and café.

The regular congregation echoed an amen chorus as Little J turned back to face the couple.

"Thank you, Little J," Aiden whispered.

"Can y'all hurry this up? I'm kinda hungry." Little J wrinkled his nose while tugging slightly on his bowtie.

The group chuckled at the boy's comment.

Then they cried while Aiden and Fisher professed their love for each other during the brief ceremony.

Then they rejoiced with cheers as the husband kissed his wife after Preacher Jeff declared them still husband and wife.

The newlyweds waited until they cut the cake before making a quick getaway. They had a date with the sun and sea with only a sailboat for a chaperone. The boat glided along the calm water on that sunny day, while couple privately celebrated the beauty of their marriage.

They may have gone about it all the wrong way, but Aiden and Fisher finally got their happily ever after.

ORANGE BLOSSOM CAFE

~☼SUNSHINE CAKE☼~
(Inspired by Phillip's sunshine)

Ingredients

- 1 package yellow cake mix (can use orange supreme or pineapple supreme cake mix)
- 4 eggs
- 2 (3.5 ounce) packages instant vanilla pudding mix
- 1/2 cup vegetable oil
- 1/4 cup pineapple juice from crushed pineapple
- 1 teaspoon vanilla extract
- 1 (11 oz.) can mandarin oranges – reserve 1/4 cup for frosting if desired
- 1 (16 oz.) container whipped topping
- 1 (8 oz.) can crushed pineapple, drained

Directions

1. Combine cake mix, eggs, 1 package of pudding, vegetable oil, vanilla extract, pineapple juice, and mandarin oranges and beat well.
2. Bake in 3 - 9 inch greased and floured round cake pans for 20-25 minutes in a pre-heated 350 degree oven.
3. Frosting: Gentle mix pudding, reserved orange segments, and pineapple into whipped topping and frost cake. Keep refrigerated.

Recipe Tip: Cake will only get better if you allow it to sit in the fridge 24 hours before serving. Also best if served with a warm smile!

~ SUNSHINE SHRIMP CAKES ~
(Inspired by Little J)

Ingredients

- 1 pound raw large shrimp, shelled, deveined and chopped
- 1 1/2 cups crushed potato chips (any flavor)
- 1 egg
- 1 green onion, chopped
- 1 finely diced jalapeno if you like a little heat
- 1 garlic clove, minced
- 1 tablespoon flour
- 1 tablespoon fresh chopped cilantro or parsley
- Juice and zest of half of lime
- Zest of one orange
- 1/4 teaspoon smoked paprika
- 1 tablespoon olive oil
- Sweet chili sauce for dipping (jazz this up with some orange zest & a splash of juice)

Directions

1. In a large bowl, add shrimp, potato chips, egg, green onion, garlic, flour, cilantro, lime juice, lime zest and smoked paprika. Using your hands, form into 8 (2-inch) or 4 (4-inch) sized patties. Cover and refrigerate for 30 minutes.
2. In a large skillet over medium-high heat, add oil. Once heated, add shrimp cakes. Cook for 3 minutes and flip. Cook for another 2 1/2 minutes or until browned. Serve with sweet chili sauce for dipping.

~ Orange Blossom Café Playlist ~

"Stubborn Love" by The Lumineers

"Try" by P!nk

"You're Love is Wild" by Zealand Worship

"Island in the Sun" by Weezer

"How Deep is Your Love" by Calvin Harris & Disciples

"Trust in You" by Lauren Daigle

"First" by Cold War Kids

"Brighter than the Sun" by Colbie Caillat

"It's Not Over Yet" by For King & Country

"Ship to Wreck" by Florence + The Machine

"Day One" by Matthew West

"Just Getting Started" by Hawk Nelson

Recipe for A Happily Ever After
Take one independent heroine and add one handsome alpha hero. Mix in a conflict, a dash of an obstacle, and allow the trouble to stir. Next, add a healthy serving of clarity to resolve any angst. Add the anticipated kiss, the tender caress, two rapid heartbeats, and combine into an awe-inspiring conclusion.

If you enjoyed this sweet little happily ever after, please check out T.I. Lowe's other stories that'll leave you smiling by the last page.

For a complete list of Lowe's published books, biography, upcoming events, and other information, visit http://www.tilowe.com/ and be sure to check out her blog, COFFEE CUP, while you're there!

She loves to connect with her reading friends.
ti.lowe@yahoo.com
https://www.facebook.com/T.I.Lowe/

Made in the USA
Las Vegas, NV
02 October 2022